THE HODGKISS MYSTERIES

Hodgkiss and the Impossible Murder

Hodgkiss and the Fortunate Flood

Hodgkiss and the General Standing Orders

PETER SINCLAIR

About the author

Peter Sinclair has spent most of his working life writing. He began reporting courts and councils in rural Orange (NSW) in the late 1950s then worked briefly for The Sydney Daily Telegraph where, because of his fluent shorthand, he was sentenced first to  report local councils then banished to the Coroner's Court.

He'd had enough of sudden death and murder when opportunity knocked and he joined the staff of a new, large weekly paper in Sydney's northern suburbs, The North Shore Times where he was soon reporting councils again.

In 1965, he climbed over the journalistic fence to work as press secretary for a succession of NSW cabinet ministers (both Liberal and Labor) until 1991. Since then, he has made guest reappearances to help out in the PR sections of government departments.

His absorbing hobby is playing the piano. He has made a number of CDs in very limited editions. The titles tell it all: Peter Murders Mozart, Wrecks Rachmaninoff and Desecrates Debussy. He says he gives them away to people he doesn't like!

He has been married to Margaret for fifty-seven years and they have two sons; Sam, who is married to Carolyn with one son, Harry, 18, and Patrick who is married to Beejai with twin boys, Jackson and Zachary, aged 13.

Published in Australia by Peter Sinclair
First published in Australia 2020
Copyright © Peter Sinclair 2020
Cover design, typesetting: WorkingType Studio

The right of Peter Sinclair to be identified as the Author of the Work has been asserted in accordance with the Copyright, Designs and Patents Act 1988.

The Hodgkiss Mysteries Volume XV
ISBN: 978-0-6450020-7-2
Sinclair, Peter
pp232

For Margaret

Author's Note

I t has been no easy task to assemble material in order to reconstruct these accounts of the extraordinary contributions which Edgar Hodgkiss made to criminal detection over the years in which he was active in the field.

Hodgkiss himself kept no records.

When he suggested solutions to investigations being undertaken by his son-in-law, Detective Sergeant Donald Burke, Hodgkiss was convinced that he was merely stating the obvious and that his contributions were unremarkable and not worthy of record.

However, this presumption that he was 'merely stating the obvious' was frequently the cause of acrimony between himself and Sergeant Burke who resented the implied slur on his own powers of observation.

Fortunately for readers of these reports (and for posterity), Hodgkiss's daughter, Esme, kept detailed records in a series of exercise books which she has kindly made available to those of us interested in researching and recording the contributions made by this unique character.

Jan Campbell-Jones, the General Manager of Kanundda Council during this testing period of its history, also kindly consented to assist by releasing relevant documents from her personal files and from council's own official records system.

Ms Campbell-Jones also graciously agreed to be interviewed and has given accounts of many of these extraordinary events from her point of view, relying on her remarkable powers of recall to provide in some cases verbatim accounts of significant conversations. In addition she has allowed us access to the many emails that passed between Hodgkiss and herself. Hodgkiss, of course, had deleted these emails from his laptop within days, or in some instances, within hours of transmission.

I am indebted also to the many members of community organisations who supported Edgar Hodgkiss in his various campaigns against what he saw as the deficiencies of Kanundda Council and who have helped me verify many important details.

Readers of these records should note that they do not appear in chronological order therefore minor temporal inconsistencies may appear.

Many incidents in which Hodgkiss played an important role have not yet been committed to paper and many others, unfortunately, will never appear on the public record.

On occasions both the innocent and the guilty must be protected.

Peter Sinclair,
Lillimoor, 2011

Hodgkiss and the Impossible Murder

Frederick Smales wedged his ample posterior into the upholstery of the carver at the top of his mahogany dining table and looked about.

At his right hand sat Kevin Anderson, bespectacled and skeletally thin. Beside Anderson sat Albert Parker, the mayor of Kanundda, known to friend and foe alike as Porker Parker. On Smales' left sat Victoria Leckie, or Vicky the Vampire as the council staff referred to her, but strictly out of earshot.

Smales could hear sounds in the adjoining kitchen which told him that his wife was preparing morning tea, shortly to be served from her oak traymobile.

He glanced at his watch, an impressive affair of two-tone gold. This meeting had already been going for too long and Smales calculated that if he brought it to an end in the next five minutes, and if they did not linger too long over morning tea, he would still have at least half an hour to spare during which he could enjoy the favours of Susan Coster, his current mistress.

Then after that pleasing interlude he would attend a meeting of the Kanundda Civic and Moral Improvement Committee which he would chair in the main meeting room at the council chambers.

Betty Clarke had rung earlier to say that she may be late for the meeting now under way and that he should begin without her. Smales snorted and decided he would be happy to close the meeting without her too.

He glanced towards the picture window with its view over the well-tended front garden and a pleasant prospect of distant bushland. There was no sign of Betty yet.

Frederick Smales thought of himself as one of Kanundda's civic leaders. Indeed this was the title which the local newspaper, the *Northern Star*, had bestowed upon him and his action group, Residents Against Planning Excesses – or RAPE as the less charitable among his political opponents referred to it.

This action group had sponsored a team of eight candidates at the recent council elections and due mainly to the efforts, and more particularly the money of the group's founding members, the team now held a comfortable majority on council which enabled Mr Smales and his well-heeled supporters outside council to monitor and where necessary adjust the directions which council took.

Cr Parker and Cr Leckie both owed their places on council to support from this group, a fact which they were not allowed to forget.

And Betty Clarke, who, Mr Smales observed, was even then pushing open his garden gate and hurrying down the path towards his front door, was also a member of the successful RAPE team. In fact Smales himself had recruited her to the cause because of her excellent reputation within the Kanundda community for frankness and integrity, a reputation she had earned during her many years as the headmistress of an exclusive local girls school.

The doorbell rang and moments later Smales heard his wife's footsteps tip-tapping quickly on the black and white tiles of the hallway as she went to answer the bell.

Moments later Betty Clarke pushed open the door from the hall and looked in timidly.

She was a tall, angular woman, softly spoken. 'I'm terribly sorry,' she twittered smiling shyly. 'Unavoidably detained. I believe that's the phrase traditionally used in such circumstances.'

Smales forced a cheery smile and hearty tones. 'That's all right, Betty. You're just in time for a cup of tea.'

Cr Clarke took her seat beside Victoria Leckie. She looked around the group anxiously and seemed about to speak, but instead looked down at the table.

This performance was not lost on Smales. 'Yes, Betty. What is it? Got something to tell us?'

Cr Clarke swallowed heavily. 'I'm afraid I have just had a most unpleasant interview.'

'Really, Betty,' said Smales indulgently. 'Perhaps you wish to share the details with us. As they say, a trouble shared is a trouble halved.'

Cr Clarke looked up to where Smales sat imposingly, smiling indulgently, elbows resting on the table. 'I'm not sure if that would be wise … not right now.'

Smales eyed her quizzically. 'Oh come one, Betty. What's the problem? Confidential is it?'

Cr Clarke nodded vigourously. 'Yes. Highly confidential actually.'

Kevin Anderson cut in. 'I don't think we have any secrets from each other in our little group, do we, Betty?'

Cr Clarke lowered her eyes. 'I think I'd rather discuss this just with Frederick first, then if he sees fit he can place it before you.'

'Nonsense, Betty,' said Smales heartily. 'As Kevin said; we have no secrets from each other. Out with it, woman.'

It was that moment that Mrs Smales chose to push open the door from the kitchen and enter the room walking backwards, pulling the laden traymobile behind her.

Cr Clarke glanced at Smales and raised an eyebrow.

Smales nodded. 'Go ahead, Betty. I don't think we have any secrets from my wife either.'

Cr Clarke inhaled deeply. 'Very well, Frederick. Well, the reason I was detained was because of a meeting I had with a fellow from the ... well, I'd better not say where he was from because that might enable you to identify him and he made me promise not to divulge his identity.'

'Anonymous information is it then, Betty.' Anderson clarified ominously, swaying to one side to allow Mrs Smales to set down a cup of black coffee before him.

'Not anonymous to me, Kevin. Confidential I would call it.'

Anderson raised an arch eyebrow, smiling lop-sidedly. 'Intriguing. And what was the nature of this ... um, mysterious, confidential disclosure?'

'It's not to be taken light-heartedly, Kevin. I'm afraid it has to do with our ... your problem here, Frederick.'

'"My problem here!" exclaimed Smales. 'What exactly do you mean by that?'

'It's to do with the development application for the unit

block on the site next door.'

There was a short uneasy silence. Coffee was stirred and sipped.

Then Smales asked quietly. 'What about it? What have you been told, Betty?'

'Frederick, I'd much rather we could discuss this one-on-one if that's all right with you.'

Smales noticed that his wife had paused in her task of distributing the cups and saucers and was looking at Betty Clarke, alarm plain on her homely features.

'Oh for heaven's sake, Betty,' Smales snapped, 'get on with it. We've all got other appointments this morning.'

Cr Clarke shrugged. 'Very well. What I've been told is this; that you, Frederick, bribed Ken Franks to recommend that council refuse the development application for the site next door.'

Smales raised an eyebrow unperturbed. 'Is that it? That's all you wanted to tell us?'

Cr Clarke nodded. 'Yes. Isn't that enough!' She added hurriedly. 'Naturally I have assumed that it's just a lot of lies, nevertheless, it is an allegation that must be confronted and denied before it is more widely circulated. Wouldn't you agree, Frederick?'

Kevin Anderson shook his head. 'I am astonished that you would even listen to such a blatant fabrication, Betty. And as for issuing a denial; I wouldn't dignify lies like that with a comment. Obviously it's just a malicious story manufactured and put about by some of our disappointed political opponents.' He turned to Smales. 'What do you say, Frederick?'

'I couldn't agree more, Kevin,' said Smales smoothly. 'I'm confident that all fair-minded people, if it ever came to their ears, would dismiss it as the obvious lie that it is.'

Cr Clarke nodded. 'I've no doubt you're right, Frederick. However, as all of us have learned to our cost, there are many people out there who don't fall into the category of "fair-minded" who would just love to spread this story if they happen to hear it. And they could do it that much more convincingly if none of us has taken the trouble to deny it.'

Smales smiled grimly. 'Yes, I agree with you there, Betty, but unfortunately I think it's fair to say that the great unwashed out there are going to believe those sorts of libels whether I deny them or not.'

'Then you're going to do nothing about it. Is that it?' Cr Clarke asked. 'I don't think that's very wise, Frederick.' She looked across the table. 'What do you think, Mr Mayor?'

Cr Parker raised both eyebrows. 'Well, of course I know nothing about any of this, but quite frankly I don't see that Fred can do much about it. What are you suggesting, Betty; that he put out a press statement denying something that no one knows anything about, except a few malicious cranks? Not very smart I'd have thought.'

'And who was it who told you this cock-and-bull story, Betty?' Smales inquired casually.

Cr Clarke shook her head. 'I'm sorry, Frederick, I can't tell you that. It was told to me in complete confidence.'

'Complete confidence, my foot,' Smales blustered. 'Something as damaging as that can't be in confidence. At the very least I'm entitled to know who told you. They're nothing but liars.'

'The fellow who told me said ...'

Smales pounced. 'So it was a man then?'

'Yes, it was a man. And that's all I'm saying, other than the man who told me seemed very sure of his facts.'

'And what have you done about it? I suppose you've been in touch with Franks to tackle him about it?'

'No, of course I haven't. That's not my job. That's up to the police.'

Smales exploded. 'Police! What the hell are you talking about, Betty. You haven't gone to the police, have you?'

'No, not yet. I wanted to discuss it with our group first.'

'Then I think you can take it as read that we don't want you taking this nonsense anywhere near the police.' He paused and looked around the table. 'Are we agreed on this?'

Heads nodded in emphatic agreement.

Cr Clarke looked around the table. 'Are you suggesting that I should forget about it? Pretend that it never happened. Do nothing at all?'

'You've got it in one, Betty,' said Anderson sharply. 'Just forget the whole silly business. It's a pack of lies.'

Cr Clarke shook her head slowly. 'I'm sorry. I can't do that. I dare say you're all right and there's absolutely nothing in it. In fact I'm sure there's not. But if word gets out that I've been informed of something like this and done nothing about it, well ... that puts me in a very awkward position, wouldn't you say?'

'That's nonsense, Betty,' said Anderson. 'In fact I would say without a shadow of a doubt that most people would say you were completely irresponsible to even think of wasting the time of our over-worked police force by burdening them with this kind of gossip, because that's all it is; malicious gossip.'

'Exactly right,' put in Cr Leckie. 'The police have better things to do with their time than go haring off down dead ends like that. And that's all it would turn out to be; a dead end; a complete waste of time and scarce resources.'

Cr Clarke nodded. 'Then I'm sure they'll have no trouble recognising it *is* a lot of nonsense and won't waste time on it.'

Smales shook his head. 'That's not the way it works, Betty. Once something like this has been officially reported the police are obliged to take it seriously and look into it. They've got no choice. They'll have to run around interviewing people, including whoever told you this nonsense. You won't be able to keep his name confidential from the police. You realise that, don't you, Betty?'

Cr Clarke nodded. 'Of course. My informant said he would be prepared to be interviewed by the police if necessary.'

'Oh, did he,' said Anderson. 'That's big of him. So this bloody deep throat of yours has actually encouraged you to take the whole business to the police, is that it?'

'No, Kevin, that's not it at all,' Cr Clarke replied with spirit. 'He said that I should take whatever action I thought appropriate.'

Anderson continued. 'You realise, don't you, Betty, that once word of this ridiculous allegation gets out – and make no mistake about it, Frederick's enemies will make dammed sure that it *does* get out – that no matter what Frederick says there will be people who will simply choose not to believe him. You know, don't you, that no matter how innocent a person is that when mud gets thrown some of it always sticks. This informant of yours knows that and that's why he's told you about it. He knows that you, being the sort of person you are, will feel you have to do something about it, like make an official report to the coppers. He's counting on that. Can't you see that? You don't think for one moment, do you, that the police are going to keep the lid on this? They're the worst people in the world when it comes to leaking and gossiping. It will be all around Kanundda in no time flat and some of the mud is going to stick for sure. You're being used, Betty. Can't you see that?'

'I'm afraid what Kevin says is true,' said Mayor Parker. 'And I should know all about mud sticking. I've had more mud slung at me than most and I can tell you that some of it always sticks although you might never have done any of the things they've accused you of.'

Cr Clarke nodded. 'I hear what you say and I know it's true. But I believe that when you go into public life, as we have, we must be prepared to take the bad with the good...'

Anderson cut her off. 'Oh come of it, Betty. This isn't a matter of taking the bad with the good. This is dirty politics at its worst, pure and simple. This is a case of someone with an axe to grind putting the knife into Frederick. This is someone getting payback and not caring how they go about it. They're just using you as their way of getting at our group for knocking them off at the last elections. Believe it or not Betty, but there are some people out there who will lie, who will resort to any sort of deception ...'

Cr Clarke cut him off. 'I know all about that, Kevin. I know that there are plenty of unprincipled people in the world and I do not intend to join their ranks and I'm afraid that's exactly what I would be doing if I simply ignored what I've been told by someone who I have always regarded as a very responsible person.'

'So it's someone you've known for a long time is it; an old mate?' Mayor Parker demanded. 'Perhaps it's even someone on council's payroll.'

Cr Clarke shook her head emphatically. 'There's no use fishing for clues to the fellow's identity. I'm not saying any more.'

'So what are you proposing to do about it?' Smales inquired quietly,

Cr Clarke hesitated. 'I'm not sure. There's someone I wish to discuss it with first. Someone who's opinion I trust.'

'You don't trust our opinion then, Betty. Is that what you're telling us?'

'No, that's not what I'm telling you at all,' she said hastily. 'But you're all too close to the problem. I need to discuss it with an outsider.'

'And would you mind telling us the name of this outsider you're planning to spill your guts to?' Anderson demanded.

Cr Clarke turned on him sharply. 'It is not a matter of spilling my guts to anyone, Kevin. I didn't ask to be put in this position but now that I find myself in it I intend to handle it my way and, I hope, with integrity. After all, when Frederick asked me to run on his ticket he said he particularly wanted me because of the high regard I was held in the community. I do not intend to do anything to let the community down and that's what I would be doing if I remain silent on this matter.'

'Do you actually believe what this fellow told you?' Smales asked. 'Because the way you're talking it certainly sounds like it.'

'No, Frederick. I do not believe that you would ever stoop to corrupting a senior officer of council to gain some kind of advantage for yourself. But at the same time I am convinced that the fellow who told me was very much in earnest and I know he will be very disappointed in me if I don't do something about it.' She paused. 'I'm sure some kind of silly mistake must have been made; that somehow there has been a misunderstanding. I am confident that ultimately things will turn out for the best; your reputation, Frederick, will be cleared of this awful charge and that will be the end of it.'

Smales stood up. 'Then there is no more to be said on the matter, is there.'

He glanced at his watch and sighed. Susan might have to

manage without him today.

'Our next meeting is a week from today,' he announced. 'Same time, same place.'

After the others had gone his wife came in with the traymobile to clear away the coffee mugs and saucers.

She said: 'I couldn't help overhearing the dreadful things that woman said.' She was close to tears. 'Oh, Frederick, I know you'd never do an awful thing like that … bribe someone. But even if it's mentioned and people start talking about it you don't suppose it could affect the … you know.'

'No I don't,' Smales snapped. 'And don't you dare mention it to anyone. Anyone at all.'

'No. Of course not. I'd never breath a word about it.'

'Good, and make sure you keep it that way.'

*   *   *

Hodgkiss was napping on the low plastic lounge on the back deck of the Burke's bungalow in a quiet backstreet of suburban Lillimoor when his daughter, Esme, pushed back the sliding door from the family room and stepped out onto the deck holding the handset from the cordless phone in the hall.

'It's for you, Dad,' she announced, thrusting the instrument towards her father. 'It's some lady.'

Still bleary with sleep, Hodgkiss took the phone. The voice on the other end of the line was faintly familiar.

'You probably don't remember me, Mr Hodgkiss,' it began. 'I'm Betty Clarke from Kanundda Council. We met over that terrible business with dear old Mr Feeney; the fellow that awful Roger Ives murdered then tried to make it look like a suicide.'

Hodgkiss nodded to himself. 'Oh yes, councillor. I

remember you very well. And I also remember every detail of that terrible crime. I was delighted to be able to play a part in bringing Ives to justice. Now, what can I do for you?'

'Well, actually, there's something I wish to discuss with you. Something of a very confidential nature. Normally I would invite you here to my home to discuss the matter but for various reasons of my own I would much prefer to consult anywhere *but* here. So would you mind very much if I was to call around to see you at a convenient moment?'

'No, not at all. When would you like to come?'

'Are you very busy this afternoon?'

'I'm no busier than usual, councillor. You could come straight away if you wish. Would that suit you?'

'Yes, it would suit me very well indeed. I'll be there in five minutes. I really appreciate this.'

It was nearer ten minutes when Cr Clarke tapped timidly on the front door of the Burke's home. Esme, who had been alerted to the visit, hurried down the hall to admit the councillor and conduct her through the house to the back deck where Hodgkiss was waiting, seated now on one of the four curved benches surrounding the red-wood table.

He rose. 'Good afternoon, councillor.' He turned to Esme. 'Would you mind bringing us some tea in ten minutes or so, my dear?'

Cr Clarke waved an arm ineffectually. 'I don't want to be any trouble, Mrs Burke.'

'It's no trouble for my daughter to make a pot of tea for a visitor,' Hodgkiss volunteered as Esme disappeared into the family room, pulling the sliding door across behind her with unnecessary force.

'Now, councillor, what is this matter of a very confidential nature that you wish to discuss with me? Or perhaps I can guess; some new example of chicanery involving the council and very likely the mayor and his little cabal of criminals.'

Cr Clarke's hands went through a fluttering pantomime designed to express mild protest. 'Oh, you're very hard on them, Mr Hodgkiss.'

Hodgkiss nodded vigourously. 'I am indeed. But not without some justification, wouldn't you say?'

Cr Clarke chose her words carefully. 'I could not in all honesty say that they always behave with the greatest probity.'

'"Greatest probity!"' Hodgkiss exploded. 'They're nothing but a band of brigands. They will stop at nothing to enrich themselves and their friends at the expense of the community.'

Cr Clarke began cautiously. 'Actually it's a matter involving one of the mayor's friends that I wish to discuss with you. Do you know Mr Frederick Smales?'

Hodgkiss shook his head. 'I don't know the man personally, but I certainly know *of* him and of his involvement with council and the way he manages to manipulate its activities, and I'm not particularly impressed. Why? What's he done now? Nothing you have to say about him could surprise me.'

'May I speak to you in complete confidence?'

Hodgkiss frowned. 'Yes. Unless of course you disclose some form of criminal conduct. As you may remember from that other tragic business, my son-in-law is a detective sergeant of police stationed at Crestwood. If you disclose some criminal act I may have to mention it to him.'

'Yes, I see.' She paused momentarily before continuing. 'I have been informed by a member of council's staff who wishes to remain anonymous for the present, that Mr Smales has bribed, or should I say attempted to bribe, a senior officer in the planning department to recommend against a particular development which, if it was to proceed, would cause

Mr Smales a good deal of inconvenience, not to say serious financial loss.'

Hodgkiss nodded and smiled. 'You wouldn't be referring to the development application for the block of units next door to Smales home, would you?'

'So you know about it.'

'I *do* read council's business paper … with a good deal of attention in fact. And I also happen to know where Mr Smales lives.'

'Well, if that application were to be approved Mr Smales would find himself living next-door to a five-storey unit block which would almost entirely overshadow his property for much of the day, particularly in winter, and also deprive him of any privacy.'

'And you're telling me that he has offered to pay off some one on council's planning staff to come up with a recommendation that council refuse the application?'

'That's exactly what I'm telling you, Mr Hodgkiss. At least, that's what I've been told.'

'Then I take it that you have already discussed this matter with Mr Smales. I seem to recall that you were one of the happy band that was elected on the ticket supported by his little pressure group, Residents Against Planning Excesses, were you not?'

'Yes, I was. And I do not regret it … not yet anyway. And of course I raised the matter with him and not surprisingly he denied it utterly.'

'Well, he would, wouldn't he? Do you believe he did it … attempted to bribe this officer?'

'I really couldn't say, Mr Hodgkiss. That's part of my dilemma.'

'Oh come now, councillor. You know Mr Smales, or you

should. You've had enough dealings with the man to form an opinion about him. Do you think he'd be capable of doing something like that?'

Cr Clarke sighed. 'That's the trouble. I *do* think he'd be capable of doing something like that without a moment's hesitation if his own interests were threatened, as they most certainly are by this development application.'

'But isn't it possible that the application could be refused in the normal course of business since the proposal could be seen to be quite out of keeping with the general tone of the area?'

'Yes, that's perfectly true, but in the past council has approved these sorts of applications, quite irresponsibly in my view, and if council rejects this particular application the fellow proposing to build this block would almost certainly go on appeal to the courts and get approval that way.'

Hodgkiss nodded. 'No doubt you're right, councillor. The way I see it is this offer of a bribe may be no more than an attempt by Smales merely to buy time until he can come up with another more permanent solution to his problem. After all, as head of RAPE he has virtual control of the council and he could persuade the ruling faction to do almost anything to block this development. He could even arrange for a heritage order to be placed on the building at present on the site next door.'

Cr Clarke nodded enthusiastically. 'Actually that is a perfectly feasible option, Mr Hodgkiss, because the existing building on that land is a very impressive old federation home of the same vintage and of a similar design to Mr Smales' home and would be very suitable for heritage listing.'

'Then it's quite probable that Smales will try to do something along those lines as a plan B if this bribery business comes unstuck and the plans look like they'll go through. Certainly heritage listing would provide a permanent solution to his problem if he could arrange it. It's a wonder he didn't think of it before he tried bribing this fellow.'

Cr Clarke shook her head. 'Heritage listing is no longer the easy option it was a few years ago. The government no longer automatically goes along with everything the council proposes.'

'And a good thing too,' said Hodgkiss. 'Too often council used heritage listing as a tool to stop any development it didn't happen to like. But we are rather straying from the point, aren't we? The point being what are we going to do with the knowledge you have acquired?'

'It is not knowledge I acquired willingly or happily, I assure you, Mr Hodgkiss.'

'Yes, I can well believe that. Knowledge sometimes is an extremely inconvenient commodity. Very well, councillor. Let's look at the situation logically. What are the various courses open to you.' Hodgkiss ticked them on his fingers. 'First, you could go to the police. Do you want to do that?'

Cr Clarke shook her head emphatically. 'No. Not if we can untangle this mess in some other way.'

Hodgkiss nodded. 'Very well. Secondly, you could report the matter to Ms Campbell-Jones and leave her to grapple with it.'

'But wouldn't she simply take it straight to the police and land it in their lap?

'No. Not necessarily. Several times in the past Jan has dealt internally with wrong-doing among councillors in the interest of preserving the council's reputation – such as it is. I would say that there would be an excellent chance that she would try first to handle the matter in-house and resolve it by negotiation rather than further degrade the reputation of local government by bringing to light yet another grubby little scandal.'

'Yes, Mr Hodgkiss, you may well be right. I know Jan sometimes operates in a rather … umm … unorthodox way if she feels it is in the best interests of the council as a whole.'

'Quite so. So she may attempt some form of um … adjustment between Smales and the person whom he has attempted to bribe and see the matter smoothed over, although somehow I can't see Smales abandoning his efforts to block the construction of this block of flats. He would see that as the ultimate insult seeing that he has spent half his life fighting developments of that kind in Kanundda.

'Then there is the third option: do nothing.'

Cr. Clarke shook her head vigourously. 'No, Mr Hodgkiss. That is not an option I would consider. I could not live with a clear conscience if, to use the vernacular, I just let the whole matter go through to the keeper and the development was blocked because of Smales' improper conduct.'

Hodgkiss nodded. 'I understand. A fourth possible course would be simply to state publicly what you have been told and let the chips fall where they will.'

Cr Clarke thought about that. 'Yes, Mr Hodgkiss …'

'Edgar, please.'

'Yes, Edgar. I think I favour that course. I could wait until the recommendation on the building application comes before council and when I speak on the subject I could just say what I know; give the facts and leave it up to the rest of council to resolve the matter. No doubt if that happens it will very soon come to the attention of the police …'

'You can be certain of that.'

' … then events will simply take their course. Of course I wouldn't name any names, that would be most unfair.'

Hodgkiss smiled grimly. 'I doubt if anyone with even the most rudimentary knowledge of local affairs would have any trouble joining the dots. After all, they'd only have to ask that most elementary of questions; who stands to benefit if the development is blocked and they'd have their answer straight away.'

'I suppose that's true enough Mr. Hodg … Edgar. But, as you said a moment ago, we will just let the chips fall where they will. Yes. I like the idea. That is what I will do. I will simply state the facts during the course of the debate on the recommendation for that building application.'

'Well, it will certainly give the reporter from the *Star* something more than usually interesting to write about. Perhaps you should alert the editor and let her know that there will be a particularly newsworthy occurrence at the meeting. In fact I think I might go along myself and watch the fireworks.'

*　　　*　　　*

Frederick Smales had just swung his low, red sports car onto the steep ramp leading down to the basement of the building where Susan Coster lived, when his mobile phone played its ringtone: *Money Money Money.*

He pulled the car into the nearest vacant parking bay, stopped, turned off the motor, picked up the phone and glanced at the caller's number.

He thumbed open the connection. 'Yes, Mr Mayor. What's the problem? I've got an appointment in two minutes and I'm going to be out of circulation for the next half hour or so. Can we make it quick?'

Parker's voice sounded unusually strained. 'I've just had a call from one of my mates at the *Star*. He reckoned that bloody Betty Clarke had been on the blower to that new girl editor telling her that there's going to be fireworks at the meeting tomorrow night so be sure to send a reporter along. She wouldn't be drawn out on any detail except to say that it'd be over a development application. You wouldn't have to be a genius to work out what she was planning to do.'

Smales pulled a face. 'Indeed you would not. Thanks for the tip. Albert.'

'So what are you going to do about it, Frederick? I mean, you can't afford to have her shooting off her silly great mouth in open council. It'll look really bad for you and just as bad for all the rest of us who were elected on the RAPE ticket.'

'Except for bloody Betty, of course,' Smales muttered bitterly. 'She thinks she can afford the luxury of a conscience. She's got a lot to learn about politics.'

'Well, you'd better have a word with her, mate, or it'll be no end of trouble for all of us. And for you in particular, especially with … er, that other business of yours coming up soon.'

'I don't know if having a word with her will do much good. I think more direct action than that might be required.'

Mayor Parker was silent for a moment. He did not like the sound of this. '"More direct action?" he inquired tentatively. 'What exactly do you have in mind?'

Smales smiled grimly. 'Not quite sure just yet, Mr Mayor, but I'm working on it. Thanks for the tip off.'

He cut the connection and pushed open the car door. Two minutes later he was slipping a key into the door of a unit on the top floor of the building.

'That you, Fred?' came a husky female voice.

'And who did you think it was? How many other men have a key to this flat?'

Susan Coster appeared at the door of the only bedroom. She had not a stitch on.

She leaned against the doorway. 'Was that a rhetorical question, Fred, or do you really want an honest answer?'

'I'm paying the tariff on this place. I reckon I'm entitled to sole rights on the occupant.'

Susan raised an eyebrow. 'Oh do you? Well, I've got news for you, Fred. You may pay the rent but that means you've got rights on the flat, just the flat ... nothing else.'

Smales decided not to pursue the matter. He hurried across the room, gathered the woman in his arms and hurried her across to the huge bed that occupied one entire wall.

She went with him willingly enough and even assisted in his undressing.

After she had removed his vest she pinched his plump chest. 'Freddy, don't you think you're a bit too young to have man boobs and love handles. Have you ever thought of giving away the grog and taking a bit of exercise? Proper exercise I mean. You'd be surprised how quickly the flab falls away.'

Smales could not tell if the woman made remarks such as this deliberately to humiliate or from a genuine concern for his well-being. He suspected the former but either way he was not amused. However, he had to concede that she was entitled to level criticism of this kind since she had taken good care of her own body which Smales found incredibly desirable since it was built more on the grand scale rather than the anorexic look favoured by the fashion industry.

Now naked, he pulled her down on the bed beside him.

'Don't you want to get under the bedclothes?' she inquired.

'No time for that today,' Smales replied and began kissing her hungrily.

Even while he was making love to the woman, Smales had an uncomfortable feeling that his efforts caused her more amusement than excitement.

When his needs were met Susan climbed from the bed, crossed to a small refrigerator concealed in a pine cupboard and poured two glasses of white wine.

Smales sat up to take the glass. He sniffed the bouquet perfunctorily, sipped the wine then set down the glass carefully on a bedside table. He rolled onto his side facing the woman.

'There's a little something I want you to do for me tomorrow night.'

Susan raised an eyebrow. 'Oh! And what if I'd already made other plans for tomorrow night?'

'Have you ... made other plans ?'

'As it happens, no. Not yet.'

'Good. So if you haven't anything else on I want you to ... I mean, I'd appreciate it if you would come along with me to the council meeting.'

Susan sat down heavily on the bed. 'The council meeting! Go with you to a council meeting? Whatever for? I don't know anything about councils or what goes on there.'

Smales waved a dismissive arm 'That doesn't matter. You don't have to know anything about it. All I want you to do is just go along and sit there.'

'That's all you want me to do ... just sit there?'

'Yes. Just sit there.'

'And what will you be doing?'

'That's no concern of yours. I always attend council meetings to keep an eye on how our councillors perform and to make sure that they vote the right way at the right times on the right motions.'

Susan nodded slowly. 'A friend told me the other day that you're some sort of local council Svengali. In fact I heard one fellow refer to you as the puppet-master. Then he had a good laugh.'

'Oh, and who was this fellow?

'Don't worry, Freddy. It's no one you'd know. Just a friend of mine.'

'Friend of yours, is he? Then I can't say I think much of some of the company you keep.'

Susan looked at him steadily. 'Yes, and actually he's said the same thing to me a couple of times about you.' She paused before continuing. 'So, what's the *real* reason why you want me along to this meeting tomorrow night? I'm sure you don't want me there just for the pleasure of my brilliant company and insightful commentaries.'

'Why do I have to give you a reason? I just asked you to come along as a favour to me. What's the problem with that?'

Susan shrugged. 'I suppose there's no problem really. I'll go along although I don't expect it will be very entertaining. Not for me anyway. I only asked why you wanted me to go along because you're such a devious so-and-so. I just wanted to be sure you aren't involving me in something shady.'

'Shady. What sort of shady things could happen at a suburban council meeting?'

'Plenty, if what you read in the press from time to time is even half true. It seems that local councils get up to all sorts of shady deals.'

Smales blustered. 'Bloody nonsense. Anyway, I'll call for you at seven and don't be late, OK?'

Susan agreed without enthusiasm.

Smales continued. 'And next Tuesday I'll be working from home again so I'd like you to drop around any time after ten and before midday. The wife will be out again at another one of her dopey book reading sessions. OK?'

Susan shook her head. 'No, I don't think so, Freddy. I didn't appreciate it last time when that woman came to the door by mistake thinking it was your wife's turn to hold the book club and you introduced me as her cousin.'

Smales frowned. 'Well, you can't blame me for that. I told you to keep out of sight but you had to come out to see who was there. What did you think I was going to do? Introduce you as my mistress.'

Susan ignored the question. 'Will you be bringing me home after this meeting tomorrow night?'

Smales grinned. 'What do you think?'

'I just wanted to be sure in case you get caught up with some of your pals after the meeting. I could always arrange other transport home.'

'That won't be necessary,' Smales snapped.

*   *   *

Jan Campbell-Jones reached for the tiny blue mobile phone on her wide, mahogany desk, selected a number from the menu and rang.

Sitting at the desk in his bedroom at the front of the Burke's bungalow, Hodgkiss took the phone from his shirt pocket and opened the connection.

'Hodgkiss. I have something for you. Are you near your computer?'

'It's right in front of me.'

'Then might I suggest you check your email. I have just

sent you a document that I am quite confident you will find of more than passing interest.'

'Really. And what fresh scandal does this fascinating document reveal. Something truly shocking I hope.'

'It's shocking enough. It provides additional information on a matter of which you are already aware in part at least; the bribery allegation involving the unlovely Mr Smales of RAPE. Betty Clarke told me that she has already consulted you on this outrageous matter and, as you will see from the document, I have just interviewed her informant in her presence.

'At this fellow's request I have represented him with an X in the transcript but if you wish to know his name I will meet you in person and provide it. I fancy that eventually the police will have to interview him anyway and he realises this and appears unperturbed at the prospect.

'What I have sent you provides a wealth of fresh and truly appalling information. I'd say that our self-important, self-styled civic leader Smales has a great deal to be worried about, particularly if Betty places her information before council tonight as she plans to.'

Hodgkiss opened his email then clicked the mouse on the latest arrival in the inbox.

'I have your email, Jan. I will be in touch when I have read it. Thanks for sending it so promptly because if any action by us is called for we may not have much time in which to consider our position and make a decision.'

Hodgkiss cut the connection and opened the attachment to the email. At once the first page of a neatly typed transcript appeared on the screen under the heading:

Interview between Cr Betty Clarke, Jan Campbell-Jones and X.

Jan Campbell-Jones: You realize, don't you X, that there is no compulsion on you to talk to us about this matter; that you don't have to tell us anything about it if you don't want to?

X: Oh yes, Jan. I realise that. But I decided to raise it with Betty because I knew it was quite wrong — what was going on. I know I don't have to tell you or anyone about it if I don't want to. Betty made that quite clear, but I don't mind. I would be quite prepared to tell the police what I know too if I have to at some later stage. This cannot simply be ignored.

JC-J: Good for you. Now, would you mind telling me just how you found out about this; about Mr Smales making an offer or inducement to Mr Franks so that he would be prepared to recommend against that development – the block of units– that is proposed to be built on the site next door to Mr Smales home?

X: Yes, I can tell you that. I found out about it quite by accident. A friend of my brother works for a bookmaker. I'd rather not give the fellow's name or the name of the bookmaker just yet, but I would if I had to … if it became necessary and the police were investigating. Anyway this fellow … this friend of my brother …he told him that Mr Smales had offered to pay the bookmaker a sum of money exactly the same as the amount that Mr Franks owes in debts for his betting on the horse and dog races.

JC-J: And how do we know that Mr Smales made this offer. What happened?

X: This friend of my brother was there when it happened; at the Travellers' Inn at Kylerbrin, in the back bar. He, that is my brother's friend, was sitting having a drink with the bookmaker when Mr Smales and another fellow came in. Smales came over to where they were sitting and introduced himself and he just said that he would be paying up for Mr Franks, probably next week, so not to worry about it. The bookmaker fellow said OK and that he had been starting to wonder what he would have to do to get his money because he had heard that Franks was particularly hard up for cash at the moment and he hadn't seen a cent of it yet.

JC-J: Is there any reason why this friend of your brother was particularly interested in this transaction. Did he know Mr Franks or Mr Smales.

X: Oh no. He didn't know them personally, but he knew about them. He knew about Mr Franks because he'd heard me talk about him more than once because we work in the same area, and of course he knew about Mr Smales because he'd read his name and seen his picture often in the local papers when he was running that group for council at the last elections.

JC-J: But as far as you know there's been no money paid over so far, has there?

X: I couldn't say about that, but I would expect that someone who's a businessman like Mr Smales would pay only on results; that is, he wouldn't be likely to actually pay over the money to a bookmaker until Mr Franks had done his bit; that is, not before the recommendation had gone to council and council had voted on it and adopted it, which would mean that the plans for the unit block to be built next door to his place had been well and truly knocked on the head, for the time being at least.

Cr Clarke: Have you any idea how much money is

involved. I mean, how much did Mr Franks owe to this bookmaker fellow?

X: That I couldn't tell you, Betty, but I was told that he seemed pretty relieved when Mr Smales came up and told him that he'd be paying up for Mr Franks. I suppose it must have been a considerable sum.

JC-J: It'd be nice if we could put a figure on it. You don't suppose this friend of your brother's could find out for us, do you? How well does he know this bookmaker?

X: I don't think I'd like to put it on my brother to ask him to do that. Besides, if there's a full police investigation that sort of thing'd have to come out anyway, wouldn't it?

JC-J: Yes, I suppose it would. Now there's one other matter that I'd like to clear up. Do we know that Mr Franks is aware of this deal; that Smales has arranged to pay his debt?'

X: Yes, I believe he is. As you know I work with Mr Franks and I heard him having a conversation with Smales. He was thanking Smales about something or other. I heard him say 'you've no idea how much trouble you've got me out of,' or something like that. Then he said: 'You know I won't be able to pay you back, or not for a long time, if ever.' Then he went on to talk about the development application next to Smales house.

JC-J: How can you be sure it was that particular development application they were talking about?

X: I know that because they referred to the builder by name. I heard Mr Franks refer to the Bathurst job and Mr Bathurst has only one development application before council at the moment. I checked on that. He said he'd already examined the Bathurst application and that he had found grounds to knock it back. Personally I found this rather surprising because I'd been the officer responsible for looking at the application when it first came in and so far as I could see it conformed to council's code in every possible way. I don't know what Mr Franks found that he could possibly have used as grounds to recommend against it.

JC-J: Just one more thing. How can you be certain that it was really Mr Smales that Franks was speaking to? Did he actually mention his name?

X: No, he didn't and I was aware of that at the time so I decided to make sure. So, as soon as the conversation was over I went out to the girl on the switch and asked her who it was that had rung through to Mr Franks and she said that the caller's name was Smales. She was quite certain of that because he'd had to wait on a bit because Mr Franks was on his other line when he rang in and the switchgirl had written down his name and number in case he hung up or dropped out and she had to call him back when Mr Franks finished his call.

Hodgkiss clicked on the reply icon and typed.

Seems like a fairly strong case although I don't think Donald would be impressed to the point where he would agree to begin an investigation. However the meeting tonight should be more than usually entertaining so I shall endeavour to be early to get a good seat because there could be quite a big roll-up if word of things has leaked out. What do you think?

EH

Hodgkiss had not long to wait before a reply arrived. *Word of this event did not have to leak out. Betty Clarke rang the editor of the Star and warned her of the coming attraction. So be very early for a good seat.*

JC-J

Hodgkiss clicked on the icon to create mail and when the format for a new email appeared he typed:

To <u>patstrong@ozemail.com.au</u>

I understand from a mutual friend that the meeting tonight of Kanundda Council will very likely be more entertaining than usual. Certainly it offers greater promise of amusement than anything on television this evening. Therefore I ask whether or not you would care to join me. I would particularly appreciate your presence as there may be a need for photography, something at which you are particularly adept with your little mobile phone. So, if you join us for dinner at, say, six, we could then be in plenty of time for a ringside seat.

EH

A reply arrived almost immediately, accepting the invitation.

Hodgkiss closed his computer and hurried down the hall to the kitchen.

'Esme, I have taken the liberty of inviting Pat for dinner this evening. We plan to attend the meeting of council which is due to start at seven thirty.'

'Oh, thanks for letting me know with so much notice,' said Esme acidly.

'But surely. ...' Hodgkiss began.

'Don't worry, Dad. It's not a problem. But it would be nice if you bothered to tell me a little earlier so I could plan.'

If it had been anyone other than Pat Strong whom Hodgkiss had invited to dinner at such short notice Esme could well have refused. But in the years since Hodgkiss and

Pat had begun their relationship Esme knew that she had a great deal to thank Pat for.

At first she and Donald had been concerned that her father's hopes for a stable relationship with the attractive widow would not be realised. But it soon became apparent that Hodgkiss's affection was sincerely returned and now he spent almost as much time at Pat's comfortable unit in an exclusive cul-de-sac in nearby Kylerbrin as he did at home.

*   *   *

'Kevin, I want you to ring around every member of our committee and as many of the rank-and-file supporters as you can muster and get them along to the meeting tonight, OK?'

'No problem, Frederick. It's pretty short notice though, and some of them might have made other plans. But just the same I'd say most would be prepared to make themselves available if you really need them.'

'Let's hope they do because we *will* really need them. There's a lot hangs on them being there tonight. Tell them that … as many as you can muster.'

'This is about Comrade Betty's plans and what she intends to say when that application comes up for debate, is it?'

'What else? She's got to be stopped at any cost … at any cost at all.'

'Personally I don't see what we can do about her at this late stage, but if moral support is what you want I reckon I can guarantee a pretty good roll-up on our side.'

'I'll be wanting a bit more than moral support, Kevin. And for God's sake be careful who you talk to because we want only people we can trust one hundred percent.'

'OK then. So I'll approach only some of the committee

and some of the more dedicated workers in the community groups. Is there anyone there you wouldn't want to be in on this … whatever it is you've got in mind?'

'I'll leave that to you, Kevin. You know them all better than I do. Only approach people who you're confident will stand by us in a crisis.'

'A crisis! Just what are you planning, Frederick? Can you give me some clue so when I ring around I can tell them what's going to be expected of them?'

'No. Not at this stage, Kevin. Just arrange for them to meet us in the Grattan railway car park middle deck about half an hour before the meeting starts. Then I'll be in a position to give them a briefing.'

'Then you must have something particular in mind then.'

'I have indeed. But to carry it out I'm going to need some cover.'

'Cover!? I really think you need to give me some idea what it is you're planning to do.'

'The less you or anyone else knows about it in advance the better for all concerned.'

'OK. Frederick. I guess you must be the best judge of that.'

'Just get them together in the car park at seven or a bit earlier if you can manage it. As many as you can. OK? Only those we can trust.'

'Good as done, mate.'

*   *   *

Pat swung the long Mercedes into the narrow laneway behind the multi-storey car park adjacent to the Grattan railway station.

'I assume you did not suggest coming here just because

there was nothing worth seeing on television,' she said. 'You don't usually come to council meetings, do you? And what was that bit about needing my photographic skills?'

Seated beside her, Hodgkiss replied: 'It is true that not being a masochist, I generally avoid council meetings. However I have reason to believe that tonight's meeting will be more than usually lively and instructive.'

Pat turned the car onto the narrow ramp leading up to the middle deck of the car park. The powerful headlights lit up the row of cars parked on either side of the deck.

'Goodness,' she said. 'I've never seen it so crowded at nighttime.'

Just then the headlights fell upon a group of men huddled together at the far end of the deck. A casually-dressed young woman stood slightly apart from the men who hurriedly turned their faces away when the headlights fell on them.

'Aha! A meeting of RAPE if I'm not greatly mistaken,' Hodgkiss exclaimed. 'And a furtive looking rabble they are too. They appear to have left their pointed white hoods at home. I wonder what that little gathering is in aid of.'

'How do you know they're from RAPE?' Pat asked as she manoeuvred the car into a parking spot then turned off the lights and motor.

'Because I recognised Smales and his creepy lieutenant, Kevin Anderson, from photographs on some of the election dodgers they put out before the last council elections. Anderson was the skinny one who turned smartly away when the lights hit them. I didn't recognise the woman, did you?'

Pat chuckled. 'As a matter of fact I did, although she had more clothes on tonight. You remember I told you that I'm a member of a book club. As you know I attend a book-reading each week and we meet alternately at the homes of the different members. That Smales fellow's wife is a member of our group. Well, one week recently I got my venues mixed up and arrived at Smales' home by mistake. He answered the door and that woman was hovering in the back ground with just a towel around her and with her hair damp as if she had just got out of the shower.'

Hodgkiss grunted. 'Really. Well, thank you for that snippet of intelligence. And did Smales introduce you to his … um, friend.'

'Actually he was so flustered when he looked around and saw her standing there in full view still dripping wet he made some half-hearted and obviously lying explanation about her being his wife's cousin. I'm sure he knew I didn't believe him.'

They climbed out of the car, Pat locked the doors and they headed for the council chambers building nearby on the other side of the Northern Highway.

Hodgkiss's hopes of securing two seats in the front row of the public gallery were dashed as soon as they pushed open the heavy double doors leading from the lift lobby to the meeting room.

The gallery already was more than half full and Pat and Hodgkiss had only just taken their places in the fifth row when the group they had seen in the car park crowded in and settled in a block of reserved seats on the other side of the central aisle towards the front of the public gallery.

They had not long to wait before the councillors filed in from a door to one side of the large chamber and took their seats around the horse-shoe shaped table which occupied most of the meeting space and which was separated from the public gallery by a low wooden rail.

On the far side of the councillors' table was a raised dais which was now being occupied by the mayor, who took his place in a central wooden chair of throne-like design and proportions.

To the mayor's right Jan Campbell-Jones took her place, eyes scanning the public gallery. When she spotted Hodgkiss and Pat she smiled and winked slowly in their direction. Other senior officers of the council took their accustomed places on the dais.

To one side of the councillors table was another much smaller table which bore a wooden sign *PRESS* where two young women and an older man competed for elbow room.

Alone, on a plain, straight-backed wooden chair, a slightly-built uniformed orderly sat centrally near a gate in the rail dividing the councillors' space from the public area.

Pat leaned towards Hodgkiss and whispered. 'Which one is Councillor Clarke?'

'She's the one sitting at this end of the table with her back to us?'

'And who's the woman sitting next to her?'

'That's Cr Leckie, known affectionately to the staff as Vicky the Vampire or so Jan tells me, and for very good reason, no doubt. She's one of Smales' acolytes.'

'And I take it that is his worship the mayor, Councillor Parker, up on the dais next to your friend Jan?'

'It is indeed,' replied Hodgkiss. 'Known as Porker Parker ... and one can see why.'

'One can indeed. Disgusting-looking little man.'

As if aware that he was under derogatory scrutiny the mayor turned in their direction, favoured Hodgkiss with a glare then turned his attention to a stack of papers before him.

He shuffled the papers about then leaned to his right, engaged in a brief conversation with Jan then picked up a small wooden gavel, rapped it on the desk in front of him and called the meeting to order.

The meeting proceeded lamely through a series of uncontentious items, recommendations from council committees, which were all approved without any discussion and on motions which, so far as Hodgkiss could see, did not appear to have been moved or seconded by any of the councillors who either sat motionless, eyes down on the papers before them or held subdued conversations with their neighbour.

It was not until recommendations from council's planning committee came up for consideration that there was a noticeable ripple of interest among the councillors and in the public gallery.

The group in the gallery, which Hodgkiss had identified as members of RAPE, was consulting their business papers and exchanging whispers and glances.

Then the mayor cleared his throat and announced: 'Item thirteen, an application to build a block of 18 home units on land at 17 Lincoln Street, Lillimoor.

'Councillors have before them the recommendation of the chief planner Mr Franks. As you see Mr Franks has recommended that this application be not approved. Is there any discussion? Yes, Councillor Verity.'

An attractive woman, seated at the extreme right end of the horse-shoe table rose. 'Mr Mayor, I understand that this application conformed in every detail to council's planning code so I am concerned that if we refuse it, as Mr Franks has recommended, the applicant will simply take us to court where we are certain to lose and once again face a very expensive bill from our barristers and solicitors as we have so often in the past in exactly these same circumstances.

'I really think it is time we began to have a little regard to the pockets of the ratepayers.' She looked around the semi-circle of other councillors most of whom appeared totally uninterested.

Mayor Parker turned to a middle-aged man seated on the other side of Jan Campbell-Jones. 'Mr Franks. Would you care to explain?'

Franks rose. 'What councillor Verity says is true. The application from Bathurst Building Enterprises *does* conform to our code in most particulars and therefore any legal action by the developer may well succeed at our expense. However, on numerous occasions in the past I have received complaints from individual councillors and from members of the public about what is called the problem of the interface; that is the situation that arises when it is proposed to build multi-unit developments beside single storey residential dwellings with all the problems of overshadowing and destroying the privacy and amenity of the adjoining homeowner or homeowners.

'I am aware that this is not specifically taken into account in our formal building code, but on this occasion. in arriving at my recommendation to the planning committee, I took into account what is obviously an area of considerable, and in my view, quite legitimate concern among many in our community, and also several councillors with whom I have discussed the matter.'

Having delivered himself of this opinion Franks sat down to a generous round of applause from the gallery.

But immediately Cr Verity was on her feet again. 'I'm sure many of us understand and sympathise with the chief planner's view on this particular matter, but as he himself conceded, this often results in great expense to the rate-payer and as things stand this council already has a legal bill approaching two million dollars incurred during just the past twelve months due almost entirely to defending usually indefensible matters just like this one. For that reason I, for one, will not be supporting the recommendation. I believe council should have greater regard for the ratepayers' pockets and reject the project.'

When Cr Verity had resumed her seat Mayor Parker looked around the chamber.

'Is there any further discussion on this item?' he inquired blandly.

Cr Clarke raised a hand then stood up.

She coughed, looked about anxiously, then began. 'Yes, Mr Mayor. There is a matter of very great importance relating to this recommendation that I feel compelled to bring to the attention of council and more particularly the public.'

Hodgkiss glanced towards the group of RAPE supporters who were all leaning forward expectantly. He noticed Mr Smales was slipping a tiny a mobile phone into the top pocket of his navy jacket behind a smartly folded white handkerchief.

Cr Clarke paused to glance towards the reporters who were hanging on her words, pens poised.

But before she could utter another syllable all the lights went out leaving the meeting room in total darkness.

For several moments there was complete silence.

Then a voice, which Jan later confirmed to Hodgkiss was that of Mayor Parker, called: 'Fergus, will you pop out and find out what's happened to the lights and see if you can put them back on again.'

Then almost at once a male voice began chanting 'lights … lights … lights.' The lone voice was soon joined by several others in loud chant.

After less than a minute the chant tailed off into a half-hearted, ragged chorus then the only voices in the chamber were the murmurings of animated conversations as people waited patiently for the lights to be turned back on.

Hodgkiss leaned over to Pat. 'That was a trifle odd, wasn't it, that chorus of lights, lights, lights! Rather juvenile, wouldn't you say?'

Pat agreed. 'Yes, I would. And it seemed to me to be coming from over there where that Smales fellow and his gang are sitting on the other side of the aisle, towards the front.'

'I believe you're right. Rather odd behaviour for group of supposedly sober citizens like that lot. Quite out of character with civic leadership, wouldn't you say? Now I wonder if ...'

But before Hodgkiss could mount any further speculation the lights came back on.

At first everyone looked about, slightly dazzled.

Then Pat nudged Hodgkiss with an elbow and whispered: 'What's the matter with Cr Clarke?'

Cr Clarke was slumped forward across the council table and Cr Leckie, on her right, was leaning over trying to get her attention by shaking her.

Unfortunately Cr Leckie's efforts apparently became too vigourous because Cr Clarke's chair swiveled suddenly through one hundred and eighty degrees and deposited its occupant on the well-carpeted floor of the council chamber near the gate in the low dividing rail.

Hodgkiss stood up, edged past Pat's knees and worked his way to the end of the row then hurried down the central aisle until he reached the wooden rail. He paused and craned his neck trying to see past Cr Verity who had now joined Cr Leckie in administering to Cr Clarke. The two women were down on hands and knees now supporting Cr Clarke in their arms and speaking to her anxiously and quietly.

Then Hodgkiss noticed Jan Campbell-Jones push back her

seat and stand. She scanned the gallery, indicated to Hodgkiss that he should stay where he was, then hurried down from the dais and around the table to where the two councillors were still ministering to Cr Clarke, apparently without result.

Hodgkiss heard Jan inquire. 'What's happened to Betty?'

Cr Leckie replied: 'I don't know. When the lights came back on she was lying forward across the desk. Then when I tried to help her sit up the chair swiveled around and she fell on the floor. I don't think she's at all well.'

'I should say she's not well. There's blood on the table and on the front of her blouse,' said Jan. 'She's been injured. Give her air.'

'I'm afraid she's more than injured,' said Cr Verity who was holding the recumbent councillor's wrist. 'She appears to have been wounded in the chest and she hasn't any pulse.'

Jan pulled a mobile phone from her jacket pocket and began thumbing in numbers.

Meanwhile, Hodgkiss had stepped over the rail dividing the gallery from the councillors' area and without waiting for Jan to finish her call he touched her on the shoulder.

'What is it Hodgkiss?' she snapped. 'I'm ringing for an ambulance.'

'I think we're going to need more than an ambulance. I may be mistaken but I think that's a firearm of some sort under the table near where Cr Leckie was sitting.'

Jan edged her way between two empty swivel chairs and stooped to make a brief but close inspection of the object Hodgkiss had indicated. Then she rose and returned hurriedly to Hodgkiss's side. 'You're right. It's a gun all right, with what looks like a silencer attached to it. Now, will you please ring Donald then go and stand at the door to the lift lobby and don't let anyone in or out. I'm sure that's what he'd want.

If they argue just refer them to me. I'm fairly sure there's a bullet hole in that poor woman's chest.'

Jan signaled to the mayor to join her and Hodgkiss stepped back over the rail, hurried up the aisle and closed the two swinging doors from the gallery to the lift lobby.

On the way he signaled to Pat to join him. 'Pat, I want you to take as many pictures as you can of everyone in this room, with particular reference to Smales and his merry men ... and woman. OK?'

Pat nodded and headed back to her seat, taking the mobile phone from her handbag as she went.

Then Hodgkiss took a phone from his jacket pocket and thumbed in a series of numbers.

'Donald, I think you'd better come at once to the council chambers. There's been an ... um, an incident.'

He could hear the frustration in Donald's voice. 'What the hell do you mean by an "incident?" What's happened?'

'I think one of the councillors has been murdered ... Cr Clarke. The one who came to see me the other night.'

'You *think* she's been murdered?'

'Well, she has no pulse; there's blood on the table where she was sitting and there's a firearm with what appears to be a silencer attached to it under the table near where she was found ... and Jan informs me that there is what appears to her to be a bullet hole in the woman's chest.'

He heard Donald sigh. 'I'm on my way. What are you doing now?'

'I'm standing at the main doors to the council chamber to prevent anyone from leaving the room.'

'OK. Give me ten minutes ... and this had better not be another one of your silly wild goose chases.'

Donald disconnected the call before Hodgkiss had time

to reply.

Then a voice at his elbow inquired: 'What are you doin' 'ere, mate.'

Hodgkiss turned. It was the uniformed officer he had seen seated at the front of the gallery when the meeting started.

'I'm making sure no one leaves the room. Police instructions,' Hodgkiss replied. 'There's been a murder. Cr Clarke has been shot dead.'

When he reflected upon the matter later Hodgkiss was convinced that the man's alarm was unfeigned. 'Murder! No. That can't be right.'

'Really? Why not? There was a pistol with a silencer found under the councillors' table and the poor woman had what appears to be a bullet hole in her chest.'

'Oh my Gawd, no!' the officer groaned.

'You lost no time turning the lights back on again,' Hodgkiss commented amicably. 'What was it? Just a blown fuse I suppose.'

'Yeah! Something like that,' said the man vaguely.

He was about to move off when Smales approached. He leaned forward and addressed the officer in a whisper. 'Did you get rid of it, Fergus?' he hissed.

For a moment the man looked uncertain, then he replied emphatically: 'Yeah. Sure, I got rid of it OK.'

'I certainly hope so,' said Smales. Then he turned and saw Hodgkiss standing nearby. 'What are you doing here?' he demanded, aware that this slight, bearded stranger may have overheard his exchange with the uniformed officer.

'I'm making sure that no one leaves the room. Police instructions,' he added.

He noticed that the handkerchief in Smales' jacket pocket

had been disturbed, possibly because the mobile phone had been pressed into service again, he speculated.

Shortly Donald arrived with three uniformed officers in tow.

*   *   *

'What on earth happened last night, Dad,' Esme asked, setting down an old, worn silverplate toast rack containing three slices of light brown toast in front of her father.

She continued. 'You rang on your mobile and the next thing Donald was out the front door like a scalded cat muttering something about you interfering again.'

'Interfering!' Hodgkiss exploded. 'Pat and I had the misfortune to be present when a very pleasant and courageous lady was murdered. What did Donald expect me to do? Ignore it? Pretend it never happened? I don't see why he should have complained. When he eventually arrived I was able to inform him promptly and in detail about what had happened. I even stood guard to make sure that none of those present at the scene of the crime attempted to decamp.'

'Well, whatever it was he didn't get home until dawn,' said Esme. 'He was still asleep when I got up.'

'Well, he's awake now.' It was Donald standing in the hall door, hair awry, his old tartan dressing gown wrapped around him and secured with a fraying cord.

'There was no need to get up so soon, Donald,' said Esme. 'I was just going to bring you a cuppa in bed.'

'Of course he has to get up,' Hodgkiss snapped. 'He can't lie around in bed all day. He's got a murder to investigate.'

Donald slid into the breakfast nook opposite his father-in-law. 'Why is it that whenever you go anywhere near that council building something bad always happens? Either something gets mysteriously stolen or someone finishes up dead.'

Hodgkiss shook his head indignantly. 'Donald, you are talking the most arrant nonsense. Most of those occurrences you are referring to would have happened whether I had been in the vicinity or not. To suggest that somehow I was responsible for ...'

Donald threw up his hands. 'I know ... I know. It's not your fault. It just happens. But somehow it only happens when you're around.'

He picked up a mug of hot, black tea that Esme had just set down in front of him. 'So, now, would you like to give me your account of what took place there last night?'

'I already gave my statement to one of your constables before I left.'

'Yeah, no doubt. But at the rate those blokes work I won't see the transcript for three days. I'd like to hear about it now ... from the horse's mouth.'

Hodgkiss bit into a piece of toast and chewed methodically.

'Instead of just reciting what happened wouldn't you prefer that I just give you the name of the murderer now and save you and the others a lot of time and trouble?'

Donald rolled his eyes. 'Dad. Who said anything about it being a murder? There's still a lot of work to be done before we can say how Cr Clarke got shot.'

'Not a murder!' Hodgkiss exclaimed. 'What do you think happened? Do you think it was an accident? Do you think that Cr Clarke was playing with the gun under the table during the meeting? That her hand slipped when she was screwing on the silencer? Is that really what you think happened? Or perhaps you think it wasn't an accident at all? Perhaps you think it was suicide; that Cr Clarke chose to shoot herself in the chest with a silenced pistol in front of the whole council and a public gallery of a hundred people. And to add to the effect she somehow arranged for the lights to be turned off and on again. Is that what you think happened? Really Donald, even the most stupid, infantile …'

'That's enough of that, Dad,' said Esme, not willing to allow an acrimonious confrontation to develop so early in the day. 'I'm sure Donald is just looking at all the possibilities.'

'But suicide or accident aren't even possibilities,' Hodgkiss protested. 'They are unthinkable.'

'Maybe,' Donald conceded. 'You reckon she was murdered, right? And now you reckon you know who did it, right? So, are you going to tell me now who did it or is this another one of those cases where you're not going to tell anyone anything until you've got it all stitched up.'

Hodgkiss shook his head. 'No. I'm perfectly prepared to name the perpetrator here and now. It was one of the men sitting in the public gallery; a self-important pompous fool by the name of Frederick Smales.'

Donald nodded. 'Yes. I rather fancied Smales'd be your first choice. I remember how you wrote all those narky letters to the *Star* running down him and his group before the council elections. What was it they called themselves?'

'RAPE. Residents Against Planning Excesses,' Hodgkiss supplied.

'Yeah! They're the ones. But no way could he have shot the woman. For a start she was shot in the chest not the in back so it would have been quite impossible for him to have shot her. He was sitting behind her in the public gallery, and where she was sitting she had her back to the gallery. Remember?'

'Of course I remember. I was at the meeting. I'm not likely to forget.'

Donald continued. 'And it was pitch dark when she was shot, right? So how could he have seen to shoot her? It's just not possible. For a start, no way could he have left his seat, climbed over the rail to the councillors' area, shot her, dumped the weapon, then got back without anyone knowing. Especially not in the dark.'

Hodgkiss nodded. 'Granted, Donald. I accept that there are certain difficulties in the way of my theory, but I can assure you that he had a strong motive to kill Betty Clarke and I have no doubt he found a way to do it.'

'Oh, yes. I've heard all about that bribery stuff last night from your friend Jan Campbell-Jones.'

'From the tone of your voice may I take it that you don't believe it?'

'I wouldn't say that I don't believe it, but so far I haven't heard a lot of proof to back it up.'

'Well, Donald, you won't find the proof you need if you don't go looking for it. And unfortunately Cr Clarke is no longer with us to tell you about it herself. Very convenient for Mr Smales, wouldn't you say?'

Donald shook his head. 'Look, Dad. This is getting us nowhere. What actual evidence do you have that Smales had anything to do with this business?'

Hodgkiss took a slice of toast from the rack and began spreading butter taken with his knife from a small cutglass dish. 'I see that I will have to begin an investigation of my own if any headway is to be made with this deplorable business.'

Donald looked up angrily. 'You'll do nothing of the sort. You will *not* begin any so-called investigation of your own. And don't you worry about Mr Smales. We've already taken a statement from him and I'll be looking personally into everything he said and did there last night.'

'Donald, that is a most simplistic approach. Do you really think for one moment that Smales will have included in his statement anything likely to draw unwanted attention to himself?'

'Of course not. But I'll have a much better picture of what happened when I've read the records of interview from all the people who were there. Including your statement.'

Hodgkiss shook his head vigourously. 'No, Donald. Even after you have read all of the statements you still won't have a complete picture of everything that happened.'

'Oh, and why do you say that? I suppose you reckon some people will have held out on us. Have you been holding out?'

'There was one thing involving Smales that I failed to mention in my statement.'

'Oh. And what was that?'

'It was something he said to that council officer whom the mayor had sent out to turn the lights back on. I think officer's name is Fergus O'Hara.'

'Oh yeah. And what was this something Smales said to O'Hara?'

'I overheard it while I was on guard at the doors from the council chamber to the lift lobby. I was standing near O'Hara when Smales came up and asked O'Hara in a whisper loud enough for me to hear: "Did you get rid of it, Fergus?"'

Donald raised an eyebrow. 'Oh! And what did O'Hara say?'

'He said: "Yeah. Sure I got rid of it OK?" I wasn't looking at them at the time because I did not wish to be overtly taking an interest in their conversation, but I can tell you that O'Hara did not sound to me at all like a man who was telling the truth.'

'OK. So what do you think *it* was; this thing that Smales was asking about?'

Hodgkiss smiled grimly. 'What indeed? If we knew the answer to that I fancy we would be well on the way to solving the murder. Why don't you ask O'Hara, or better still, ask Smales?'

Donald shook his head. 'Even if there *was* something in it they'd deny that any such conversation took place, wouldn't they?'

'Undoubtedly. Which means that we will have to identify and recover this particular object, whatever it is, without their assistance.

'And how do you propose to do that, might I ask?'

'I can't say … not yet anyway. But you may be sure I will be working on it. And I would suggest most urgently, Donald, that you put out of your mind any idea that that poor woman's death was anything other than murder.'

'On this occasion I have to agree with you, Dad. Suicide and accidental death really don't cut the mustard. So, unlikely as it seems, it must be murder. But if you think that someone in the public gallery shot her … well, so far as I can see that's just plain impossible.'

'I agree that's the way it seems at present, Donald, but I am confident that on this occasion what at first seems impossible will, in the end, turn out to be the only feasible solution.

'Ask yourself this, Donald: if someone shot her from the front, that is, someone sitting at the official table where the mayor, Jan and council's senior officers are to be found, or any one of the other councillors seated around the table fired the fatal bullet, then it seems impossible that all those nearby could have failed to notice that something untoward had happened, even with the lights out. Even silenced guns make some sound. And a murder victim, when struck by a fatal bullet, probably will not die in total silence. So someone must have heard something, unless …'

'Unless what? Donald demanded.

Hodgkiss shook his head. 'My word. I am slow today. It was all that chanting.'

'Chanting! What are you talking about, Dad?'

'Didn't anyone mention the chanting in their statements? No. Possibly not. Come to think of it I didn't mention it either.'

'Someone may have mentioned chanting but I haven't had time to read all the statements yet.'

'Well, what happened was this; as soon as the lights went out … or just moments later … Smales and his group, or that's where it seemed to come from, and Pat will bear me out on this … began a sort of rhythmic chant of "lights … lights … lights."'

'And how long did this chanting go on for?'

'Only a minute or so. Not long at all, then it sort of tailed off rather than end abruptly, much as it had started.'

'And is there anything else you've forgotten to mention?' Donald asked sarcastically.

'Yes. There was one other thing. After the lights went out and before the chanting started I heard someone, I believe it was the mayor, tell Fergus O'Hara to go and see what had happened and to turn the lights back on.'

'OK? Anything else?'

'No. But wait a moment, there was just one more thing that no doubt will prove to be important. Pat and I saw Smales and a group of his supporters huddled together in the middle deck of the Grattan railway car park as we arrived for the meeting. I would say that it is highly likely that Smales was giving them a pep talk or possibly riding instructions on what to do at the meeting because it is obvious, is it not, that the chanting was designed to cover the sound of the shot. Oh, and one other thing I forgot to mention; Smales mistress was among the group.'

'His mistress! How do you know that? And who is she anyway?'

'I suggest you ask Pat about that. She may not have mentioned it in her statement but she should have a photo of the woman in question. I asked Pat to take photos of as many of the people in the chamber as possible after the lights came back on.'

'Did you indeed. Well you might have told me before. I'll need all of those photos to make sure that we didn't miss taking a statement from anyone.'

Hodgkiss shook his head. 'I really don't think that all these statements will amount to much. It seems that people often forget to mention the most important aspects of a matter when they make formal statements.'

'Not wrong there, Dad. And that certainly applies to you,' Donald said tartly.

*   *   *

Donald had no sooner left for the police station when the phone rang.

It was Pat. 'Hodgkiss. There's something I didn't tell you … or Donald either.'

'About last night?' Hodgkiss asked. 'Donald has just been telling me off for omitting one or two trifling snippets from my statement. What did you leave out? Nothing significant, I trust.'

'No. It's not about anything that happened last night. It's just some information about Smales; personal information.'

'Excellent. Out with it then. I hope it's bad for Smales,'

'I should say it is. It's something his wife told me when I was at her place recently for one of our book readings. The two of us had just gone out into the kitchen to prepare morning tea for everyone and she said she'd tell me something if I promised never to mention it to any one else. Anyone at all. Ever.'

'I think in the present circumstances you would be justified in passing on any information, whatever it is, if you believe it could have any bearing on Councillor Clarke's murder.'

'I should say it is particularly relevant if we really think Smales had anything to do with it.'

'And we most certainly do, don't we?'

'Yes, I suppose we do.'

'So, out with it. What's this deadly secret?'

'Well, Mrs Smales told me under seal of the confessional that about a month or so ago an envelope arrived with a government crest on it and it turned out that Smales has been recommended for an Australian honour. Not the highest one, but he's pretty chuffed about it and of course so is she.'

'I should think they would be, although what the man really deserves is a public flogging rather than some kind of honour, considering all he's done to damaged our suburbs through his idiotic ...'

'Never mind all of that Hodgkiss. Don't you see, the fact that he could face public exposure for bribing that council officer gives him an excellent motive to put poor Councillor Clarke out of the way.'

Hodgkiss nodded thoughtfully. 'You're right, of course, Pat. He and his wife must be terrified that the offer of the honour would be withdrawn, as it certainly would be, if there is any kind of serious scandal about him in the press. Yes. It gives him an excellent motive.'

'And there's one other thing' said Pat. 'In spite of him being a bit of a rat nevertheless we should be careful not to give him some kind of unpleasant shock unnecessarily if and when Donald or any authority ever confronts him.'

'Oh. Why do you say that?'

'Well, I think he must have a weak heart.'

'A weak heart! How do you know that? Did his wife tell you that as well?'

Pat shook her head. 'Oh no. But I had occasion to visit their bathroom during one of the book readings and while I was powdering my nose I happened to notice a medicine bottle with his name on it on the shelf near his toothbrush. It contained some sort of heart medicine.'

'This medicine; did it have a name? There are all sorts of compounds designed to treat heart conditions.'

'It was some compound of atropine. I looked it up on Google and atropine is used to treat various heart conditions. It's made from Deadly Nightshade.'

'Was that it … just atropine? You said it was some compound.' Hodgkiss pressed.

Pat frowned. 'I think there was something before the atropine part. I think it might have been homatropine or something like that?'

'Homatropine? I've never heard of it, but then I wouldn't, would I, not being a chemist? Anyway, I'll warn Donald when I see him and suggest that when he arrests Smales for murder he do so politely and not raise his voice for fear of bringing on an attack of the vapours. Meanwhile, I suggest that you ring Donald and bring him up to date on the Australian honours business. I'm sure he'll find that of considerable interest. You might as well tell him about the atropine too.'

When he had cut the connection Hodgkiss opened his internet browser and typed in *atropine*.

After reading three articles on atropine and related compounds Hodgkiss closed his browser with a self-satisfied smile.

'Well, that puts an interesting and very different complexion on Smales' activities in this particularly nasty business,' he said aloud to himself.

'It also suggests an answer to the question: 'What was the thing – the *it* – that Smales was referring to when he asked Fergus O'Hara: "Did you get rid of *it*, Fergus?"

He smiled smugly, then caught his reflection in the mirror behind the bedroom door. The smile faded.

'But the problem is; will Donald believe me?'

*   *   *

When Donald arrived home for dinner he found Hodgkiss on the back deck, reading, slumped uncomfortably in a striped director's chair.

Hodgkiss slipped a bookmark between the pages and wriggled awkwardly out of the chair as Donald mounted the shallow steps up from the driveway.

'Did Pat contact you about last night's events?' he asked.

'D'you mean did she ring up to tell me about all the things she'd forgotten to put in her statement? Yes, she did.'

'Puts rather a difference complexion on things, wouldn't you say?'

'In what way, exactly,' said Donald, heading for the sliding door to the family room.

'In what way?' Hodgkiss repeated angrily. 'Surely you're joking, Donald. It puts Smales right in the centre of the frame.'

He followed Donald through the family room and down the hall towards the kitchen where Donald crossed to the small refrigerator under the bench, stooped and took out a can of beer.

He pulled the tab from the beer can and took a long draught. 'Because of that knighthood business, d'you mean?'

'It wouldn't be a knighthood. Just an Order of Australia. And a fairly lowly one at that, no doubt. But it gives him a very strong motive to keep Councillor Clarke quiet.'

Donald smacked his lips. 'Maybe.'

'There's no "maybe" about it, Donald. If he was involved in a bribery and corruption scandal before the awards are announced there is every chance that the offer of an honour would be withdrawn and he knew it.'

'All speculation, Dad. Not an atom of proof anywhere.' He vented a loud belch.

Hodgkiss looked away in disgust.

Donald continued. 'Pat also sent me some photos by email. What am I supposed to learn from them? And she said something else about Smales; that he might have a weak heart. What am I supposed to do about that; hold his hand while I question him, not that there's much to question him about. He's done nothing criminal so far as I can see; certainly not on the information I have so far.'

'Do you think not?' Hodgkiss demanded aggressively. 'Well, may I make a few constructive suggestions?'

'Well, you're going to anyway, aren't you, so get on with it.'

'I have given the matter considerable thought and it seems to me that in order to bring this matter promptly to a successful conclusion there are five questions that need to be answered.

Donald chucked. 'Five! Only five, Dad. You disappoint me.'

Hodgkiss ignored the gibe. 'First, who turned off the lights in the council chamber?'

Donald grunted; 'Come off it, Dad. That's a no brainer. Do you think we haven't been asking around about that? What do you know about it … if anything?'

'Will you allow me to continue with the other questions then perhaps we can come back to that one because I may be able to help you find an answer to your "no brainer".

'The second question is: who told that person *when* to turn the lights off and on again?'

'The third question is: What was the *it* that Smales referred to in his conversation with Fergus O'Hara that I overheard?'

'Yeah! Well, we've already been over that and we're none the wiser.'

Hodgkiss ignored this interruption. 'The fourth question is: Why was Mr Smales using a compound of atropine?'

'Well, we know that too, don't we? He had a bad heart.'

'Really? Have you checked that with his doctor?' Without waiting for a reply Hodgkiss continued: 'And the fifth question is: what did Smales say to the gathering of his cronies in the car park before the meeting?'

'Is that all? No more questions?' Donald asked caustically. 'Well can we return to the first one: the one about who turned out the lights. You reckoned you can tell me who it was.'

Hodgkiss shook his head. 'Really, Donald. You don't pay attention to anything I tell you. I said no such thing. All I said was that I may be able to assist you finding the right person, or words to that effect.'

'OK, then. Let's have it. How can I find out who it was?'

'It should not be difficult. It boils down to this; I happened to be looking in Smales' direction just seconds before the lights went out and the last thing I saw before everything went dark was him putting his mobile phone in the top outside pocket of his jacket.'

'So you reckon he'd been on the phone giving the signal to whoever it was who turned the lights out, right?'

'Makes sense, wouldn't you say, Donald? It would also account for the timing, because it was at exactly that moment that Councillor Clarke was on her feet and about to begin her speech that would have resulted in Smales' exposure as someone who offered bribes to secure a personal advantage. Very damaging in the public's mind, and to his prospects of receiving an honour from the government.'

Donald nodded. 'OK. I suppose that's worth following up although it may not be all that simple to get access to his personal phone records. I'd certainly need more than what you've just told me.'

'Well, that's your problem, Donald, but I believe it should present few difficulties if you really apply your mind to it.'

'It may come as news to you, Dad, but I have to work within the law. Police officers can't run off to the phone companies just on a whim and demand to look at the private records of their subscribers. Besides, we don't even know which phone company he's with. Now, is there anything else that you just happened to forget to put in your official statement?'

Hodgkiss nodded. 'Yes. Actually there is one other thing I should have mentioned if I had thought of it at the time. It's about Smales' handkerchief.'

'Smales' handkerchief! What about it?'

'Well, as I mentioned a moment ago, just before the lights went out I saw him put his mobile phone away in the top pocket of his jacket, just behind the handkerchief. At that time the handkerchief was neatly folded. Later, after the lights came back on and when Smales was having his whispered conversation with O'Hara, asking whether he had got rid of *it*, I noticed that his handkerchief had been disturbed. It was no longer neatly folded.'

'Right. And what do you conclude from that?' Donald demanded.

'Surely that's obvious. He had taken his phone out again to use it and in so doing had disturbed the handkerchief.'

'Well, that's not much help unless we can get our hands on his telephone account.'

Hodgkiss held up a hand. 'But wait a moment. Perhaps I'm wrong. Perhaps it had nothing to do with his phone. Perhaps he wanted the handkerchief for another purpose.'

'To blow his nose, d'you mean?'

'No, Donald. Not to blow his nose. If you were going to shoot someone what would you use to avoid leaving finger-prints on the weapon?'

'Gawd, that's drawing a long bow, isn't? You happen to notice he's used his handkerchief so you decide he used it to hold a gun to shoot someone, not that he's simply used it to blow his nose.'

Hodgkiss shrugged. 'Very well, Donald. Ignore my suggestion if you wish, but ...'

'I didn't say I was going to ignore it. But the problem with your theory is that Councillor Clarke was shot in the chest, not in the back.'

'Really, Donald, that is a most superficial objection. Don't you think it likely, or at least possible that Councillor Clarke may have turned around towards the public gallery when the lights went out, particularly once the chanting started.'

'Then you think that the chanting might have been intended to attract her attention?'

'That's possible, surely, as well as to cover the sound of the shot.'

'Yeah. I suppose it is. But even so, and if she did turn around, how could Smales or anybody else in the public gallery have shot her. When the lights are out in that room it is bloody dark in there. We tested it. There are no windows in that meeting room to let in even a glimmer of light. If she was shot from the public gallery whoever did it must have been able to see in the dark, even if she turned around to oblige them.'

'Now, that is a very interesting idea, Donald. I suggest that you give it some serious thought.'

'What? The idea that she was shot from the public gallery by someone who could see in the dark?'

'Yes, exactly.'

'Well, if she was shot from the public gallery whoever did it must have stood up or they would have risked shooting the people in front of them. Right?'

Hodgkiss nodded. 'Yes. Unless the people in front of the shooter obligingly ducked down to give him – or her – a clear shot at the victim.'

'Not necessarily. No one would have to duck down if the shooter was sitting in the front row or if they stood up to do it, would they?'

'That's true, Donald, however I can tell you that Smales was not seated in the front row. He was seated in the third row in the middle of a block of his supporters. But Pat's photos should settle that question.'

'Yeah. They could come in handy. At least they'll help us settle who was sitting exactly where.' He nodded. 'And I see what you mean about needing to find out what Smales and his gang were talking about during their little confab in the car park. If your theory is right and Smales did it, then anything he said to his mates before the meeting started should give some clue to what he had in mind to do at the meeting.'

'Yes, Donald. Although I must caution you not to expect too much from such a line of questioning since I suspect that Smales briefing to his troops would necessarily have been of a fairly general nature because I doubt very much if he could have relied upon all of them to stand by him if he was the subject of a murder charge. So I fear that you will discover that nothing he told them would have been of such a nature that it could provide direct, damning evidence against him.'

'So what do *you* think it was all about ... the briefing?'

'I suspect that it was little more than an appeal to follow his lead if anything untoward happened.'

'And how do you suppose the gun got where it did; under the table? It would have been a lucky toss to get it to land almost at the poor woman's feet.'

'Yes, Donald, no doubt that's true. But it didn't have to be a lucky toss, as you put it. It really didn't matter where the gun landed, did it? Actually the fact that it finished up under the table neither complicates nor simplifies the inquiry, because the killer could not have been sure where it would land in the dark or seriously believed that the police would accept either suicide or accident as a serious option.

'So the point of throwing the gun into the councillor's area on the other side of the dividing rail was merely a device to draw attention away from the true location of the killer.'

Donald sighed. 'You may be right, Dad. Obviously we've still got a long way to go.'

'True, Donald. But I guarantee that your journey will be considerably shortened if you concentrate your efforts on my five questions.'

Donald shook his head and raised the beer can once more. 'OK, Dad. First up I'll see what I can do about getting a look at that Smales character's phone account.'

Hodgkiss nodded approval. 'An excellent place to begin.'

*   *   *

'It's a bloody good thing you didn't say too much to the troops about what you had in mind, Frederick. They're scared out of their wits as it is, most of them.'

'You don't think they suspect anything then, Kevin?'

'No. They know only what they were told; that we wanted them to follow your lead if anything unusual happened, and believe it or not the cops haven't even asked them about the chanting business yet.'

'You mean they don't even know about it?'

'Oh no. They know about it because I mentioned it in my statement. I figured it'd look a bit odd if I didn't and they found out about it later. No. What I meant was that none of our lot's mentioned to the coppers that we'd discussed in advance about backing up anything you said or did. I think the coppers might just assume that it was a spontaneous thing, which it was in a way. You just started chanting "lights, lights, lights" and the others simply joined in. End of story.'

'Good. And let's hope it stays that way. Actually, with hindsight there was no need to brief our troops in advance about anything. They probably would have joined in anyway. Now, what about Fergus? Do you think he'll be OK? Have the coppers spoken to him yet?'

'Yes. They've spoken to him; they've spoken to everyone who was there. I have to tell you, Kevin, that I don't like having to depend on people like Fergus.'

'Couldn't agree more. But in the circumstances we didn't have a lot of choice. After all, it's his official job to enforce order in the chamber during meetings if things look like getting out of hand. It would have looked more than a little odd if we'd tried to have him replaced with someone else just for the night. What exactly did he tell the police? Do you know?'

'Well, according to him he didn't tell them a thing except his name, rank and serial number.'

'And did he get rid of the … the you-know-what?'

'Yes. Or he said he did.'

'Then let's hope he has … really.'

'I asked him especially about it at the first chance I got after the lights came back on and he said he did.'

'Yeah! Well, let's hope he was telling the truth. It just struck me that he's the sort of simple-minded yob who might take it into his head to hang on to the thing; keep it to play with .Or maybe sell it because it must be worth a few bob. It would never do if the coppers got their hands on it and tracked it back to you. It'd blow the whole thing wide open.'

'You're right there. I'll have another word to Fergus and make sure that he really *has* disposed of it.'

'Apart from that it seems everything went … fairly well. I overheard that the detective from Crestwood, Burke's his name I think, saying to one of the uniform coppers that it looked like it might have been an accident.'

'Really! Then let's hope that he doesn't change his mind. Even if they start to suspect one of our lot I guess their biggest problem is going to be working out how come Betty was shot in the chest when we were all sitting behind her in the gallery.'

'Yes. That and how could anyone sitting that far away see well enough in the dark to shoot her. That was a stroke of genius. Dumb coppers will never tumble to that … not in a month of Sundays.'

A short silence.

Then Smales added: 'Let's hope not anyway.'

*   *   *

'At least I've managed to persuade Donald that it was neither suicide nor an unfortunate accident.'

Hodgkiss was seated on the end of his bed, the handset from the cordless phone in the hall pressed to an ear.

At her desk in the general manager's office at the front of the Kanundda Council Chambers building, Jan Campbell-Jones sat, a polystyrene mug of black coffee in one hand and her tiny blue mobile phone in the other.

'I should think it would have taken anyone with half a brain no time at all to rule out those two options,' she said. 'It had to be murder although I must confess there are one or two difficulties even about that. I mean, however did the assassin know where to aim in the pitch dark? He could have killed anyone firing off a gun like that.'

Hodgkiss nodded his head furiously. 'Ahha! That is indeed the question. All other considerations are peripheral. Nothing can be achieved until that central question is addressed and answered reasonably. How did he know where to aim?'

'Doubtless Donald is busily addressing that question as we speak.'

'That among others. In fact I took the liberty of offering him a list of five questions for his consideration; questions which, when answered, will, I believe, undoubtedly lead to a rapid solution.'

'Only five questions? Really, Hodgkiss, I am bitterly

disappointed in you. I can think of at least a dozen without trying. I suppose you have rung up to try out these questions on me.'

'Not all of them. For the present I want you to help me to find the answer only to the first question.'

'Which is?'

'Who turned off the lights?'

'And what makes you think I will be able to help you out on that one. After all, I was in the chamber at the time and know no more about the matter than you … probably less.'

'Granted. We were all at the same disadvantage, except of course for the person who turned off the lights.'

'Then how can I help?'

'You can help me find a particular phone number; the number of the person who rang whoever it was that turned off the lights.'

'And whose number might that be. No. Let me guess. Mr Frederick Smales.'

'My, my. You *are* on the ball today.'

'And what makes you think that the unctuous Smales is the person involved.'

'Because quite by chance I happened to be watching him during the few seconds just before the lights went out. He used his mobile phone, placed it in the top pocket of his jacket then almost at once the lights went out. I find that sequence of events irresistibly suggestive.'

'Could have been coincidence.'

'So it could. But could it also have been a coincidence that the lights went out at the very moment that Betty Clarke was about to begin her address to council that would have ended in Smales' disgrace. Too many coincidences there, wouldn't you agree?'

'I certainly would. So you want me to find Smales' mobile phone number? Is that it?'

'If it's not too much trouble. I think it highly likely that you have it somewhere in your vast administration. After all, he is a person who has many connections with council; he is chairman or member of numerous council committees, is he not, and a regular confidant of many of your councillors. In the course of his interfering activities he must be in almost daily contact with many of your senior officers.'

'Not just senior officers, Hodgkiss. He rings me so often that sometimes I have to tell Jenny Cope, my PA, to tell him that I'm not in or at a meeting. I'll look up the number and email it to you. OK?'

'Excellent. Then Donald will have one excuse less to delay his investigation into Smales' involvement in this matter.'

'I take it that once Donald has particulars of Smales' phone he can gain access to the record of his calls.'

'Yes, although he made much of the legal difficulties in the way of doing so; privacy etc. However, if he dilly-dallies I have sources of my own who would make the search for me, but it would be better if Donald did it officially. Oh, and one other thing. Did you happen to make a note of the precise time when the lights went out? I may need that to pin-point the timing of Smales' phone call to his accomplice. I have only an approximate idea of the time because once the lights came back on I was busily engaged elsewhere.'

'As were we all. And as to the exact time the lights went out; as it happens I can tell you that to the second because in the little kitchen adjacent to my office I have one of those early types of plug-in electric clocks where, in order to start it again after a power failure, you have to twist a knob on the back to re-start the motor. I haven't bothered to re-set it yet so it is still showing the exact time when the power stopped on this floor. I will email you the time as well Smales mobile number. Happy hunting, Hodgkiss!'

*   *   *

Half an hour later Hodgkiss was just passing the cordless phone in the hall on his way to the bedroom when it rang. He scooped up the handset as he and continued on his way.

It was Donald. 'Well, I've just interviewed that O'Hara character.'

'And?' Hodgkiss inquired, sitting down on the end of his bed.

'And nothing.'

'What do you mean "and nothing?" He must have told you something.'

'All he told me was that when the lights went out the mayor called out to him to go and find out what had happened and turn them back on again. He reckons he did that and nothing more.'

'What about his conversation with Smales?'

'There never was a conversation with Smales, or so he says.'

'He's lying of course.'

'Maybe so. But it's going to be the devil's own job to prove it.'

'And what else did he tell you?'

Nothing much. But there was one other thing. As I drove up to his house I saw Smales get into his car and drive away.'

Hodgkiss shook his head ruefully. 'So he beat you to it. Do you happen to notice if Smales was carrying anything when he left?'

Donald paused. 'Yes. He was carrying a bag.'

'What sort of bag. Was it a deep carry-bag, an overnight bag; how big was it?'

'I'd say it was an overnight bag.'

'Which means that we can no longer expect to find at O'Hara's home the object – the "it" — which Smales was referring to in the conversation that I overheard. We must find some other means of establishing *it's* nature. Will you be home for lunch, Donald?'

'Yes. I'll be coming by about twelve. Why?'

'Because I want you and I to call on Mr O'Hara at home. I believe I know how we can persuade that gentleman to tell us exactly what it was that Smales took away in his overnight bag.'

'The hell you can!" Donald exclaimed. 'How do you propose to do that?'

Hodgkiss smiled smugly. 'Wait and see, Donald. I suggest you trust me. After all, how often have I failed you in the past?' Before Donald could reply he hurried on: 'But I can't stay chatting. I have some shopping to do.'

He cut the connection and hurried back down the hall towards the kitchen, returning the handset to its cradle as he passed.

In the kitchen Esme was stacking the breakfast things in the dishwasher.

'Esme, do you know if that sporting goods store in the Grattan Shopping centre is still in business? So many of those smaller shops have closed down lately.'

Esme looked up. 'Yes. I walked past it yesterday. It's the one with all the rifles in the window, isn't it?'

'That sounds like the place. I need to make an urgent visit there before Donald comes home at midday. Could you drive me there?'

'Well, I was going up to the Grattan shops anyway. Are you ready now?'

'I am indeed. I'll be waiting for you in the car.'

It was not a long shopping expedition and Hodgkiss and Esme were home well before noon, Hodgkiss with his purchase from the sporting goods shop in a deep carry bag.

When Donald arrived home shortly before noon he found Esme and Hodgkiss seated at the redwood setting on the back deck finishing off a plate of cheese and tomato sandwiches with their crusts cut off.

'Hey, aren't you going to save some for me,' he said as Hodgkiss reached for the last sandwich.

'I'll make you another round,' said Esme, pushing back the curved bench and heading for the sliding door to the family room. 'I won't be long.'

'I'd say that leaves us just enough time to visit Mr O'Hara and be back here in time for you to enjoy lunch. He lives only five minutes away. I checked his address in the phone book.'

Donald agreed with poor grace.

'What have you got there?' he asked as Hodgkiss slid into the front seat of the unmarked police car and settled the carry bag onto his lap.

'This,' said Hodgkiss, patting the bag, 'is the item that will enable us to persuade Mr O'Hara to tell the truth about what happened.'

From previous experience Donald knew better than to demand a more complete explanation. He started the motor and backed carefully down the driveway.

Five minutes later they pulled up in front of a small, well-kept cottage in a back street in West Rosbury.

O'Hara, in a singlet and shorts, was mowing the front lawn with a push mower.

When Donald and Hodgkiss approached he stopped mowing and looked up. 'You back again. Whaddaya want now? I've tol' you everythin' I know.'

'Not quite everything, Mr O'Hara,' said Hodgkiss, stepping forward.

'An 'ho are you?' O'Hara demanded. 'Hey! Didn' I see you at the council meetin'?'

''You did indeed, Mr O'Hara. In fact I was standing almost at your elbow when Mr Smales and you held a brief, whispered conversation. Well, not actually a conversation. More a short exchange of words.'

'Nah! I never spoke to Mr Smales. Not at the meeting.'

'That's not true, Mr O'Hara. In fact I have made a sworn statement to this police officer that Mr Smales approached you near the swinging doors at the rear of the council chambers shortly after the lights came back on and he asked you if you had got rid of … *it*. And after a moment's hesitation you assured him that you had. Now, that was not the truth, was it, Mr O'Hara … not then?'

O'Hara looked away evasively. 'I don' know what you're talkin' 'bout.'

'I think you do,' said Hodgkiss He reached into his carry bag and drew out a black metal object, elongated, like a deformed telescope.

He held it out towards O'Hara.

O'Hara's mouth fell open. 'Where'd you get that?' He asked, stunned. Then realising his mistake, he hurried on: 'But that's not it, anyway.'

Donald pounced. 'It's not what?'

O'Hara hesitated then replied doggedly. 'I've got nothin' more to say to either of you.'

'I don't blame you for deciding to hold your tongue for the

time being, Mr O'Hara,' Hodgkiss continued pleasantly, 'but just one more question, if you wouldn't mind; when you went to turn the lights back on, where did you go and what did you do? There's no harm in telling us that, surely?'

'No. I don't want to talk about anything to do with what happened. OK?'

Donald shook his head. 'I'm afraid you're going to have to tell us a great deal more than you have so far. In fact I think it'd be a good idea if you came down to the police station with me now, so would you like to go inside and get dressed. I'll wait for you here.'

When O'Hara had gone inside Donald turned to Hodgkiss. 'Nice one, Dad. And you reckon it wasn't him that turned the lights back on.'

Hodgkiss shook his head. 'I doubt that very much.'

'Then who do you reckon did?'

Hodgkiss reached into his shirt pocket and drew out a neatly folded slip of paper. 'That I cannot tell you, but this is the number of Smales' mobile phone. Once you have obtained access to his phone records you will be able to find out who he rang seconds before the lights went out. I have also made a note of the precise time when the lights went out on that floor of the building.'

Donald shook his head. 'I am not going to risk asking how you found out this number because it might come back to bite us both later.'

Hodgkiss frowned. 'That is nonsense, Donald. Smales' mobile phone number is not a state secret. He has broadcast it far and wide among many of the senior staff at Kanundda Council, including Jan, with whom he has had regular contacts on what he presumptuously regards as his business.

Jan also was able to ascertain the precise time the blackout started.'

'And you reckon it wasn't O'Hara who put the lights back on?'

'No. I think it is far more likely that whoever turned them off also turned them back on.'

'But how would he have known when to turn them back on?'

'I would say that he had prior instructions from Smales to turn them back on after a given period had elapsed, say two minutes; time enough for Smales to have done his deadly work.'

'So you still reckon it was Smales that shot her?'

Hodgkiss frowned. 'Donald, do you seriously doubt it. She was shot, was she not? We now know that while the lights were out Smales gave O'Hara this device, a night vision monocular scope which enabled him to clearly make out his target, shortly before the lights came on again. We know, too, that Councillor Clarke was planning to expose him as a man who engages in bribery of public officials which would jeopardize his elevation to the ranks of holders of Australian honours. So Smales had means, opportunity and motive. Pretty conclusive, wouldn't you say?'

Donald was loath to concede a victory to his father-in-law. 'I'll say it's pretty conclusive when we've got everyone involved behind bars.'

*   *   *

'Bad news, Frederick. That copper's taken Fergus in. God knows what that dopey bastard will tell him. We've got problems, mate. Big time.'

'It may not be as bad as you think, Kevin. I didn't tell Fergus anything important and I wasn't wrong about him wanting to hold on to the night vision scope. Luckily I got it away from him just in time. That copper arrived just as I was leaving. That was a near thing because sure as hell they'd have scared the pants off him and he'd've handed it over if they'd pressured him. If he tells them that I gave him the thing to remove from the council chamber I can simply deny it and say he's having an aberration. He's not the sharpest tool in the shed, you know.'

'And Charles Cooper rang me a while back. The coppers want him to call at Crestwood Police Station to make a further statement about what you told them at our meeting in the car park before we went over to the council chambers.'

'Now that could be a problem. What did you tell Charles?'

'Just to say that you told them that they should support you when you gave them a lead on anything; for example to jeer if council came up with any dopey motions that we disagreed with; just our way of letting them know that we didn't agree with something they were doing. Not necessarily anything to do with the lights going out.'

'Well done, Kevin. Have you told the others to follow that line if they're asked?'

'Yeah! I managed to reach all of them so it should be OK provided they hold their nerve. What about the fellow who turned the lights off and on. What was his name? Hopeless Harry you called him.'

'There's no chance in the world they'll ever get onto him. He wasn't even rostered on duty at the time. Besides I've told him to keep out of sight for a week or two. He's owed about a month's leave. I'd say we're safe there. Now, what about my … um, friend, Susan. What are we going to tell the coppers about her, Kevin? We can't say she just turned up by accident, can we?'

'Don't worry. I've thought of that. The coppers think she was there with someone else. Just the same I don't understand why you brought her along. She's nothing but a loose cannon. Another problem we don't need.'

'Couldn't agree with you there, Kevin. But we needed all the cover we could get. It wouldn't have worked if I'd finished up sitting next to just some member of the public. I had to have our people all around me otherwise we couldn't have done it.'

'Maybe you shouldn't have gone ahead with it anyway.'

There was a short silence.

'It wasn't just I that went ahead with it, Kevin. We knew what was happening ... both of us.'

But instead of receiving a reply Smales found himself holding a dead handset.

*   *   *

'What were those five questions of yours again, Dad?'

Donald was sitting opposite Hodgkiss in the pine breakfast nook. They each had a mug of black tea in their hands and a large aluminium teapot with red Bakelite handles rested on the table between them.

Hodgkiss blew across the surface of his tea then looked up. 'Why do you want to know that, Donald? Do you think you have all the answers?'

Donald nodded eagerly. 'I reckon I might. Now, what was the first one?'

'The first one was: "who turned off the lights?"'

Donald nodded. 'Right. Well, I got a mate of mine at the telephone company to run a check on Smales' account and ...'

'Tsk! Tsk! Naughty, naughty, Donald. Quite illegal.'

'Maybe, but I'll be able to get a warrant and do it all legally when we're a bit further down the track.' He took a mighty gulp of tea. 'Smales made a call just a few seconds before the time Jan gave for the lights going out and it went to a guy who works for the council named Harold Robbins – no relation to the author.'

'And you got the information about Robbins' phone number from Jan, I take it.'

'That's right. She checked the mobile phone records of all employees and although he wasn't supposed to be on duty that night he obviously was there.'

'You say "obviously", Donald. But what will you do if when you interview Robbins he says that his friend Smales rang him at home to inquire after his sick wife?'

'Won't wash, Dad. He left his fingerprints all over the switches in the fuse box. His prints were already on record for an old assault.'

Hodgkiss nodded. 'Well, that takes care of the first question. What about question two: who told him when to turn the lights off and on again?'

'I reckon there'll be no trouble over that one. When this Robbins guy finds that he's been involved in a murder he'll spill the beans and name Smales.

'Now, your third question, if I remember correctly, was what was the item Smales referred to in the conversation you overheard him having with O'Hara. Well, we know that, don't we? It was that see-in-the-dark telescope thing you got hold of, right?'

'A night vision monocular I believe they are called.' Hodgkiss said pedantically. 'And it wasn't cheap, Donald. I expect the department will recompense me for the cost.'

'Yeah! Well, we'll cross that bridge when we come to it.' He took a gulp of tea. 'I still can't figure out what put you on to that thing.'

Hodgkiss smiled smugly. 'Yes, so I've noticed. Which brings us to the fourth question: why was Smales using atropine? Obviously you don't have the answer to that one yet?'

Donald nodded. 'Yeah! That's the only one I haven't got the answer to yet. So give, Dad. What did this atropine stuff have to do with it all?'

'Do you know what atropine is used for? Pat thought it was used in some medications for people with heart disease. No doubt she's right and atropine is used for that purpose in some forms.

'But it has another use. It is used by optometrists to make the pupils of your eyes dilate so they can be more thoroughly examined. But one internet site I came across suggested that atropine could improve your night vision once your pupils were dilated.

'I've no doubt that Smales experimented with it for that purpose, found it didn't work and bought the night vision monocular instead.

'Now, that leaves only the fifth question; what did he say to his little gathering in the car park before the meeting? Do you have any further information on that?'

'Yes, I do. I had all those who took part in the meeting come to the station to make further statements and they all trotted out the same story. Smales had asked them to back him in any sort of action he took during the course of the meeting if council did anything they didn't like; anything that ran contrary to RAPE policy. They were to take their lead from Smales or Anderson and that's what they did when they started that chanting business. That's what they all said.'

'And you believe them?'

Donald shook his head. 'Not a word of it. For one thing they all had the story off too pat. Some of them even used the same words in places. It just wasn't believable.'

'And have you taken further statements from them … all of his henchmen who were sitting around him in the public gallery? You can identify them from Pat's photos.'

'We've taken extra statements from all the guys at the car park gathering but we still have to have a chat to his hench-woman. Do you remember her?'

'Yes. A rather good looking piece as I recall. I think per-haps Pat could tell you a thing or two about her.'

'Nothing complimentary I gather.'

'Far from it. Apparently she is Smales mistress. He enter-tains her at his home while his wife is out.'

Donald's eyebrows shot up. 'Does he really! You don't hap-pen to know where I can find her, do you? We need to talk to her.'

'Couldn't any of the others in that little group tell you who she was?'

Donald shook his head. 'They all remembered her being there, but when we asked who she was with they all reckoned she wasn't with them and she must have been there with someone else.'

Hodgkiss sneered. 'A likely story. But if you want to know how to contact her I think Pat may be able to help.'

'Well I need to know. And quickly.'

Hodgkiss swamped down what was left of his tea and slid sideways out of the breakfast nook.

'Then I'd better get onto Pat now and see what we can do,' he said.

'Wait just a moment,' Donald called anxiously after his

father-in-law's retreating figure. 'I don't want the pair of you to get up to anything illegal.'

'Perish the thought, Donald,' came the reply from halfway down the hall. 'Would we do a thing like that?'

'Too bloody right you would … the pair of you. So watch your step.'

In his bedroom Hodgkiss sat down at the table in front of the room's only window and took the mobile from his shirt pocket. He thumbed the keypad and waited.

'Pat. Do you have any plans for the remainder of the day?'

Pat Strong had been relaxing on the low plastic couch on the veranda off her upstairs bedroom when the phone rang.

'No, Hodgkiss, nothing that can't be put off. Why?'

'Donald feels the need to urgently identify the young woman in one of the photos you took of the jolly gathering in the council chambers after the shooting; the lady whom Smales identified to you as his wife's cousin on that occasion when you called at his home by mistake.'

Pat nodded. 'Oh, her. Well, we never believed the cousin story for a moment, did we.'

'Certainly not. But now we need to make a more reliable identification.'

'Oh. And how do you propose to do that?'

Pat listened attentively while Hodgkiss spoke.

Then abruptly she sat upright. 'No, Hodgkiss. No. No way will I be involved in something like that. That's cruel.'

Hodgkiss smiled to himself. 'Yes, I thought that may be your reaction. So if you want no part of it then I suggest you just drive me there and leave me to do the rest.'

'Hodgkiss, this is a wholly reprehensible exercise.'

'So you say. But you'll drive me there, won't you, and save the expense of a taxi.'

'Yes, I will, but only because I'm going there anyway for one of our book club sessions.'

'Excellent. I will be waiting out on the nature strip in ten minutes. Will that suit?'

'I suppose it will have to, won't it?'

*　　　*　　　*

Fifteen minutes later, with Hodgkiss seated beside her, Pat pulled the big Mercedes over and parked outside a large Federation bungalow in one of the best streets in Lillimoor.

Hodgkiss nodded towards the house next door. 'And it is there, next door, that some greedy developer had planned to build his block of units that Smales so heartily objected to. Can't say I blame him really. A highly inappropriate location for units, wouldn't you agree?'

'Maybe so, Hodgkiss, but I doubt if you would have resorted to bribing a servant of the council in order to prevent it. I'm sure you would have found some legal way around the problem if you had felt the need to stop it.'

Hodgkiss nodded as he climbed from the car. 'Very likely.'

Together they strode up the crazy paving pathway that led to the front door of Smales' home. Hodgkiss swung the knocker and stood back.

'Let's hope he's at work,' he said as footsteps could be heard advancing rapidly on the other side of the door.

There was the rattle of a safety chain and the door was pulled back.

A woman of middle height and age stood in the doorway. She smiled at Pat. 'You're a little early, dear,' she said. Then her glance fell on Hodgkiss.

'Does your friend want to join our little group? She inquired politely.

Pat coughed. 'No, I'm afraid not, although he may at some time. He's a great reader. For the moment the reason I came a little early is because my friend, his name is Edgar Hodgkiss, by the way, wants to ask you about ...'

Mrs Smales recoiled. 'Not the Edgar Hodgkiss who writes those awful letters to the *Star*. I know Frederick would be most displeased if I told him that I had been speaking to Mr Hodgkiss.'

Hodgkiss decided it was time to enter the conversation. 'Well, Mrs Smales, I am sorry to have to tell you that it is in connection with your husband that I have called.'

'Then I think you had better come back later when he is at home.'

Hodgkiss shook his head. 'No. That would not do at all. You see I need you to assist me to identify a friend of his.'

'Then you'll have to ask him about it. I don't know many of his friends.'

'But I suspect you will know this one – seeing that she is your cousin.'

Hodgkiss stepped forward and thrust towards Mrs Smales one of the photos Pat had taken in the council chamber. 'That lady there,' he said laying a finger on the only woman in the print.

Mrs Smales glanced at the photo then turned angrily to Hodgkiss. 'That's not my cousin.'

Hodgkiss feigned amazement. 'Not your cousin! Are you sure, because your husband assured Pat that she is. You see Pat called here one day to attend a book club meeting. But she had the wrong day. It was the turn of one of the other ladies in your group to host the reading. When your husband opened the door to Pat that lady was standing behind him in the hall half naked, her hair wet as if she had just come out of the shower. Apparently he felt compelled to explain her presence, so he told Pat that she was your cousin.'

Mrs Smales pulled the door open. 'Do you mean to tell me that he brought that slut here … to my home?!'

Hodgkiss nodded. 'There seems to be no doubt about that.' For confirmation he turned to Pat who nodded unwillingly.

Mrs Smales stepped to one side. 'Then I think you had better come in … both of you.'

When they were seated in a comfortable lounge room at the front of the house Mrs Smales continued. 'I'm sure that you, Pat, were not deceived by Frederick's lies. That woman is his mistress. She has been for quite some time now. Certainly she has lasted longer than most of them.'

'Would you mind giving us her name and address? The police want to speak to her in connection with the death of Betty Clarke.'

'I will be very pleased to give you any information I can about that her; not that she is any better or any worse than any of the others.' She hesitated, then turned to Hodgkiss. 'What exactly is your interest in this matter, Mr Hodgkiss?'

'My sole interest is to see that justice is done. As it happens the officer in charge of the investigation into Betty Clarke's murder is my son-in-law, Detective sergeant Donald Burke. At present Detective Burke is anxious to identify the lady in this photo and seeing that Pat had taken the photo and knew of her association with your husband we thought it best to approach you first rather than your husband which may have proved rather awkward.'

'Well it will certainly prove more than awkward for Frederick. I suppose you know about his forthcoming honour?'

'Yes , Pat mentioned that, but only after the murder had been committed and because it was apparent that it provided a strong motive for murder ... something that could not be kept from the police.

Mrs Smales nodded. 'Well, everything has backfired grandly, hasn't it? There'll be no honours now ... not once he's in jail.'

'So you believe that he was involved in the murder plot?'

'Involved in it. I would say he planned it.'

'Do you have any proof of that?'

'No, I suppose not. I wish I did.'

Hodgkiss tugged at his neatly trimmed grey beard. 'Perhaps you *do* have proof, but just don't realise it.'

'Whatever do you mean by that, Mr Hodgkiss?'

'Do you know that your husband has in your bathroom a bottle of a substance that is a compound of atropine?'

Mrs Smales nodded. 'Yes. I saw it there a few days ago. I wondered what he wanted it for.'

'Do you know if he has ever used it?'

Mrs Smales smiled. 'Yes, he has. Strange that you should ask.'

'Strange. Why? What happened?'

'It was funny as a circus. I saw him put some drops from that bottle in both his eyes then he hurried along to the little spare room at the back of the house on the south side and pulled all the blinds down to make the room as dark as possible.

'Then for a while he just sat there in a chair, waiting for the stuff to work I suppose.

'After about fifteen minutes he got up, turned off the lights and tried to walk around in the dark.'

'How do you know that, Mrs Smales? You weren't in the room with him at the time, were you?'

'No. But I was just outside in the hall, listening. I could hear him blundering around inside, bumping into things, knocking over furniture. Cursing and swearing. Anyway, later on I asked him what had he been doing in there and he said that the eye drops were no good because he couldn't see a thing. Apparently they help you to see better in the dark, or so he thought.'

Hodgkiss stood up. 'Would you mind if I took the bottle away with me. I think my son-in-law may want it as evidence.'

Mrs Smales nodded cheerfully. 'By all means, Mr Hodgkiss. It's down the hall, second on the left. Go through the bedroom to the *en suite*. It's there. Help yourself. Oh, and while you're there have a look in the long drawer in the bottom of the chest of drawers. If you look under his shirts you'll find something else that might interest you.'

Three minutes later Hodgkiss returned, a tiny medicine bottle in one hand and in the other a night vision scope, held gingerly in a handkerchief.

'Would you have a plastic bag somewhere, please, Mrs Smales? I wouldn't want to smudge any fingerprints on this thing.'

'A pleasure, Mr Hodgkiss.' Mrs Smales bounced out of her chair and headed for the hall. At the door she stopped and turned. 'And tell your son-in-law that I will be down at the station first thing in the morning to make a full statement.

'I'll show the cheating bastard!'

*　　*　　*

Donald arrived home just as the six o'clock news was ending. When Hodgkiss heard the unmarked police car pull up in the driveway he climbed hurriedly out of his wingback armchair and headed for the kitchen.

Esme, who was cutting up carrots on the chopping board, looked up when he came in. 'For heaven's sake Dad, give Donald time to catch his breath before you start quizzing him, will you?'

'Very well, my dear,' said Hodgkiss, sliding into the breakfast nook. 'It will be interesting to hear just how Donald has resolved this supposedly impossible murder.'

'Impossible murder,' Esme exclaimed. 'Why do you call it an impossible murder.'

'Because that's what the aficionados of the whodunit genre would make of it; how can the murderer, sitting behind his victim, contrive to shoot her in the chest from a distance of five metres and all in a pitch-dark room. Sounds pretty impossible, wouldn't you agree?'

When Donald came in through the laundry Hodgkiss continued: 'Anyway, there won't be much he can tell me that I don't already know.'

Esme shook her head and looked angrily at her father, but decided not to comment.

But Donald had heard the remark. 'Is that what you think, is it, Dad? That you know the lot?' He stooped and pulled a can of beer from the bar fridge, ripped off the tab and took his place opposite Hodgkiss in the breakfast nook. 'Then let's hear you tell it all as it happened ... in detail. See how smart you really are.'

Hodgkiss shook his head. 'Donald, there is no need for me to go through the whole awful rigmarole. You know already that I am familiar with the general outline of this appalling business. I would be obliged if you would fill in those details which only you will be aware of at this stage, having had the advantage of interviewing the principal players or reading their statements.'

Donald took a hearty tug on his beer. 'Yeah! Well I had a very interesting visit from that Smales fellow's chief lieutenant, Kevin Anderson. D'you know him?'

Hodgkiss nodded with little enthusiasm. 'Yes, I know Anderson. And a very unpleasant piece of work he is, too. I suspect he would prove to be an excellent source of information if he has decided it is in his own interests to roll over.'

'You're not wrong there, Dad. And he *has* rolled right over. As soon as he heard that O'Hara had come clean and made a statement he decided that the game was up and that he should start to look after number one; not that it'll keep him out of jail.'

'So by now you must have a detailed knowledge of the entire operation since Anderson must have been up to his ears in planning the whole thing.'

Donald smiled. 'Oh no. He had nothing whatever to do with planning it. Not when you hear him tell it anyway. The way he described things makes it perfectly clear that it was all Smales' work and he was just a bit player. But then he *would* say that, wouldn't he.'

'Undoubtedy.'

'He said Smales planned it all like a military operation. It went like this: first there was the meeting in the railway car park when the supporters were lined up and told about supporting anything Smales did at the meeting … follow his lead if he started anything.

'He also stressed the importance of remaining seated at all times, no doubt so he'd have a clear shot when the lights went out.

'Smales carried the gun with the silencer already attached into the meeting room under his jacket and Anderson took in the night vision scope in a brief case and under duress, or so he said.

'Next step; when the lady councillor got up to speak Smales rang the guy who turned out the lights.

'Then as soon as the lights went out Smales starts his chant, and his little gang of supporters, as instructed before hand, join in … Lights, Lights, Lights, to cover any sound that the gun might make.

'Then a few seconds after the lights went out the person sitting next to Betty Clarke, a woman by the name of Victoria Leckie, reckons that Clarke turned around to face the gallery when the chanting started … natural enough I suppose.

'Then Leckie reckoned she heard Clarke give a kind of grunt and she spun back around and fell forward across the table.

'No doubt Smales, who had his night vision scope and gun at the ready, just stood up and shot her.

'When all the chanting started that Fergus O'Hara character walked up the aisle to the end of the row where Smales was sitting. He'd been working for council for years and knew every inch of that room like the back of his hand.

'So when Smales had done the deed he knew exactly where O'Hara would be waiting. He handed him the night vision scope to take away with him when he went out supposedly to turn the lights back on as the mayor had asked him.

'Of course O'Hara had been told not to bother about the lights because Smales had already instructed the bloke who turned them off to turn them back on again after two minutes.

'But of course O'Hara had to dispose of the night vision scope. He hid it in locked in the cubby hole he used in the council chambers and removed it the following day and took it home.

'Smales tossed the gun in the direction of the councillors'

area where it lobbed and came to rest under the table.

'It didn't matter where it finished up exactly because when it was found in the councillors area it would distract attention from where the shot was actually fired.

'By the time the lights came back on everything was back to normal, except for Cr Clarke, who was found shot dead facing the wrong way, that is away from where the bullet had actually been fired.'

Hodgkiss nodded. 'Very neat, but incredibly complicated, thus almost certain to fail when one has regard to the calibre of those upon whom Smales was obliged to depend for a successful outcome.'

Donald nodded. 'You're not wrong there, Dad. Even most of his own group couldn't drop him quickly enough. It seems he wasn't very popular, even among his own alleged supporters.'

'Hardly surprising. He is a nasty, arrogant piece of work. One can only pity that poor wife of his.'

Esme turned from the sink. 'Well, that's a novelty, that is, you being sorry for someone's wife. Let me tell the pair of you, it's not only that fellow's wife who's had a lot to put up with. I suppose you think I enjoy the two of you running in and out at all hours of the day and night and bickering over practically everything that happens.'

Donald turned to protest, but he caught a warning glance from Hodgkiss and the two decided to accept whatever criticism Esme had to make.

Much of it, they knew, was quite justified.

*   *   *

Late the following morning Pat rang just as Hodgkiss was

returning from the nearby Lillimoor Oval where he and been exercising his dog. Rupert.

He had just detached Rupert's lead and removed the harness when the phone rang.

'Are you free for coffee in ten minutes?' Pat asked. 'There's someone we know who wants to talk to you.'

'And would you mind telling me who this someone is? I don't like mysteries.'

Pat exploded: 'You don't like mysteries! What utter rubbish. You thrive on mysteries! You'd be dead without some sort of mystery to beat your brains over. I'll pick you up in ten minutes.'

When Hodgkiss was settled beside Pat in the big Mercedes she leaned over and kissed him firmly on the lips.

'So that you don't have to suffer any more suspense; the mystery person demanding your presence is none other than the horrendous Smales' unfortunate spouse, Yvonne.'

Hodgkiss nodded. 'And when were you speaking to Mrs Smales?'

Pat slipped the selector into Drive, pressed the accelerator and the car slid away from the kerb. 'She rang this morning to say that she wouldn't be doing any more book readings until further notice. Then she said there was something she wanted to talk to you about and could I arrange it.'

'And you don't know what it's about I suppose?'

'Yes, I do, but I'll let her tell you. She'll be waiting for us at Frendz.'

Five minutes later Pat reversed the car into the kerb outside the little café in West Lillimoor where Hodgkiss could see Mrs Smales already seated at one of the round tables under an umbrella in the courtyard at the front of the building.

She stood as they approached.

'Thank you so much for coming, Mr Hodgkiss,' she said, extending a hand. 'And you too, Pat.'

Hodgkiss shook the hand and the three settled around the tiny table, knees touching.

After the young waitress had taken their orders Hodgkiss asked: 'Now, Mrs Smales … er, Yvonne. What was it that you wished to discuss?'

Mrs Smales glanced from one to the other. 'Actually I just wanted you to know about something … something I've decided to do.

'First of all I should mention that I've decided to leave Frederick, or more accurately, I have asked Frederick to leave me … to leave the house.'

'It's your house then, I take it,' said Hodgkiss.

Mrs Smales nodded. 'It certainly is. Frederick had very few assets of his own when we married and that situation has changed little in the twenty years since.

'The small accountancy practice which he inherited from his father went steadily downhill because Frederick concentrated more on council matters than in keeping abreast of the continual changes in the law which would have enabled him to make the business prosper. He relied too much on his staff who he paid very poorly with predictable results.

'Anyway, I mention that only by way of background.

'I have decided to be realistic about my future.

'There is no doubt in my mind that I will be facing the future alone. Indeed I would have been on my own even if I had not asked Frederick to go, because it seems from what our solicitor has told me, that Frederick will be spending a good deal of time in prison in the years ahead. Therefore I must make decisions about how I am to live and where.'

'Where? You're thinking of moving, then?'

Mrs Smales hesitated. 'No. I would prefer not to move. I like the location; close to the shops, all my friends live nearby, and there's the reading group ...'

Hodgkiss smiled, shaking his head. 'Your husband would not approve if you are planning to do what I think you have in mind.'

'I'm sure you're right, Mr Hodgkiss. Luckily I do not have to consult him about it.'

Pat began: 'You don't mean you're going to ...'

'Yes, Pat. I'm going to redevelop. I'm going to knock the house down and build units like they're planning next door. I suppose the builder's chances of getting approval might have improved now that all this business about the bribery has come out.

'Then when the units are all finished I'm going to live in one of them ... the best one; the penthouse on the corner facing north-east.'

'Good for you, Yvonne,' said Pat.

Mrs Smales turned to Hodgkiss. 'You're a bit of an expert on local government matters, aren't you Mr Hodgkiss? Do you think council will let me do it?'

Hodgkiss nodded. 'I don't see why not. I assume your land is big enough to accommodate such a development. And I know the zoning allows it. I doubt if you would have to bribe anyone to recommend approval. RAPE would certainly oppose it and try to get their lackeys on council to vote against it. But I have a feeling they won't be as amenable to following orders as slavishly as they have been in the past. I would say you'll have no trouble getting your plans through.'

'And jolly good luck to you,' said Pat.

Then their coffees arrived.

Hodgkiss and the Fortunate Flood

'Her name is Mina Cumberland. I went to school with her mother,' Pat Strong explained as she backed the long Mercedes neatly into a parking bay directly outside Frendz Coffee Shop in West Lillimoor.

'And it looks like she's here already,' Pat added, looking over her shoulder. 'That's Mina sitting outside under the umbrella.'

Edgar Hodgkiss wriggled around in his seat to look out the rear window. 'The blonde with curly hair? Is that the one?'

'That's her,' said Pat, unbuckling her seat belt. 'Now, I realise that it's a rather improbable story she's told me, but try to be a little sympathetic. She's really upset about it.'

'Honestly, Pat. I am not entirely insensitive, you know,'

said Hodgkiss peevishly. 'I have been known to display an appropriate level of sympathy when the occasion requires it.'

Pat raised a sceptical eyebrow. 'Really! Well, from what I can remember displays of appropriate compassion on your part are pretty few and far between.'

Hodgkiss ignored the sally and climbed out of the car to join Pat on the footpath.

'Well, she looks normal enough,' he conceded out of the corner of his mouth as the woman rose, smiled and waved cheerfully in their direction.

'She *is* normal enough,' said Pat. 'It's just this one thing that's really got under her skin.'

After the introductions were made and the three settled at the tiny table with their coffee and cake ordered, Pat began: "Well, Mina. I haven't said a word to Edgar about your ... experience. I thought it best if he heard it straight from you.'

Mina glanced at Hodgkiss then looked down at her hands resting clenched on the table. 'It's all so ... well, silly, that it's almost embarrassing to talk about it. But seeing that Pat said you might be interested to see if you could help work out what's happened ... well, here goes.'

She took a deep breath. 'A couple of weeks ago I was reading through the local paper when I noticed in the real estate for sale pages an advertisement for a house that I lived in when I was a small child.

'I decided, just out of curiosity, to go along on the inspection open day and have a look, and also because I had to visit someone who lived nearby anyway so I wasn't really going out of my way.

'Then when I entered the house the strangest thing happened: I could remember only two or three of the rooms at the front of the house although I'd actually lived there for … well it must have been about a year … maybe a bit less.

'I could remember the kitchen very well and the little bedroom off the kitchen, the front hall and a tiny bathroom. Nothing else. On the open day I walked all through the house but couldn't remember a thing about any of the other rooms.

'Of course even things about the few rooms I *could* remember had changed, like the paint, the wallpaper and the furniture. But I could remember the rooms themselves, the shape and the smell of them – quite clearly.'

Hodgkiss asked. 'Was it a very large house? Were there many other rooms … rooms you couldn't remember?'

Mina frowned in thought. 'It wasn't a huge place and when I went through it the other day I made a note of the other rooms; the ones I couldn't remember. There were three other bedrooms – I assume they were bedrooms because the house was empty and there wasn't a stick of furniture in the whole place. And there was a living room and a large bathroom towards the rear of the house and I couldn't remember a thing about any of them.'

'Perhaps they had been added on since you left, or parts of the house were rebuilt or something like that,' Hodgkiss suggested.

Mina shook her head emphatically. 'No. I particularly asked the agent who was in charge of the inspection about that, and she said the house had been built more than fifty years ago and it was still in original condition. She was quite sure that there had never been any major additions or alterations to the place. She even showed me on the wall a framed architect's drawing of the original floor plan and four elevation drawings which proved that nothing had changed since the place was built, not structurally anyway.'

Hodgkiss nodded. 'And you want to understand why it is that you can't remember the rest of the house; just a few rooms in the front? Is that the problem?'

Mina nodded but said nothing.

'Is it important?'

'Yes it is … to me. Very important.'

'Why is that? I mean, you were only a small child at the time. Surely it isn't unusual that a child would not have a detailed recollection of each and every room in a house where she lived. How old were you when you were living there?'

'I was about five when we moved out. Perhaps a little less. I'm not positive about that.'

'We? Who is the "we?"'

'My mother and I.'

'I take it you have put these questions to your mother.'

Mina shook her head. 'Mum died not long after we left the place. I went to live with an aunt after Mum died.'

'And might I enquire about the whereabouts of your father at the time?'

From the corner of his eye Hodgkiss caught a warning movement of Pat's hand.

He continued hastily. 'That is if it's not indiscreet to inquire?'

Mina smiled wanly. 'It's not indiscreet, Edgar, it's just that I can't be very helpful on that subject. You see Dad disappeared about that time.'

'About *what* time?'

'About the time we moved away.'

'And where did he disappear to … do you know?'

Mina shook her head. 'No idea. We never heard a word from him. Vanished into thin air.'

Hodgkiss shook his head. 'No, Mina. People do not vanish

into thin air. Even on those occasions when they may wish to. Were the police notified of his disappearance?'

'Oh yes. I've checked on that. Of course I didn't know it at the time but Mum reported Dad as a missing person but we never heard anything back … or not that I know of.'

'So you never found out if there had been any developments … that the police had discovered anything … unsubstantiated sightings, bank withdrawals … things like that?'

Mina lowered her eyes. 'Not a word. But I suppose the police may have discovered something and tried to pass it on but we moved around a lot about that time, so I suppose it's possible the police may have found out something but couldn't find us to let us know.'

They paused while their coffees and a plate with three friands were set down on the table.

Hodgkiss added three sachets of raw sugar to his coffee, stirred, picked up the mug carefully with both hands and sipped cautiously. 'Then it's your father's disappearance that is worrying you, is it; possibly even more than your curiosity about the house?'

Mina shook her head vigourously. 'Oh no. That's not it at all. It's the business about not remembering the house, or most of it. I can't understand why I have such a clear recollection of just a few rooms at the front of the house and the rest of the house … nothing. A complete blank. Don't you think that's really strange?'

Hodgkiss ignored the question. 'Don't you have any ideas of your own about it … any theories at all?'

Mina reached into a large black leather bag resting against her chair and drew out an old, small photo.

'That's Mum and I taken outside the house,' she said.

Hodgkiss wiped his fingers on the small paper serviette

in his lap and took the photo in both hands carefully by the edges.

It was in black and white and there was something intensely bleak about it; almost sinister.

In the middle distance a woman, apparently in her thirties, stood in front of an ordinary weatherboard house, holding the hand of a small anxious-looking girl, standing close beside her. Both were frowning into the camera.

A little distance behind them and to one side, a dark-haired man of about forty stood side on, looking over his shoulder, an unpleasant smile on his face.

'Who's the man?' Hodgkiss asked.

Mina shook her head. 'I don't know his name. He was a friend of Dad's ... or I *think* he was a friend.'

'You think?'

'Well, I remember that he was around the house a lot so I suppose he was a friend ... or an acquaintance. But I seem to know that Mum didn't like him being around. In fact I have the feeling that she was afraid of him. I'm sure she was.'

Hodgkiss nodded. 'I can tell *that* from the photo.' He paused. 'Do you associate this man with your ... situation ... your problem?'

'D'you mean do I think he's in some way connected with why I don't remember the rest of the house? Yes, I suppose I do, but I don't know why or how.'

Hodgkiss glanced at Pat then turned to look directly at Mina. 'Do you think, perhaps, that he was involved in some way with something bad that happened there ... in that house, in the rear section, in the rooms you cannot recall.'

'Yes. Actually I'm quite sure of it. Although I couldn't tell you why I think that.'

Hodgkiss smiled grimly. 'You don't need to. It is perfectly

understandable, surely.'

Mina turned, shocked. 'Understandable. How?'

'Because you are convinced that something happened in that house … something terrible which accounts for why your memory has wiped clean all recollection of the inside of those other rooms and the bad events that you knew took place in them.'

Mina looked aghast. 'No. You think that man abused me or something like that. But that's not what I think at all. I'm sure I'd remember if something like that had happened … if that man had done something awful to me.'

'The mind can play extraordinary tricks on us when it has to protect its own sanity. Do you have another explanation?'

Mina looked at him, open mouthed. She shook her head. 'No, I don't. But I assure you that I never thought … no, not for one moment that it was caused by anything like that.'

Hodgkiss shook his head slowly. 'No, Mina. That can't be true. You must have considered that as a possibility. Be honest, now. You did, surely.'

Mina inhaled deeply and closed her eyes. 'No, Mr Hodgkiss, I promise you. Besides, there's no proof … no evidence even, that anything like that happened. It's just too awful even to think about. And if it *had* happened then surely I would have remembered something.'

'Not necessarily. But let us move on.'

Hodgkiss picked up the photo again.

'Have you any idea who took the photo. I suppose you'd remember if it had been your father.'

Mina shook her head. 'I've no idea who took it. I'd completely forgotten about the photo until after I'd visited the house and started looking through some of the old things I'd inherited from Mum … things I hadn't look at for many years or, in the case of the photo, things I'd never seen before as far as I can remember. I thought there might be some clue somewhere about the missing rooms.'

'It's quite clear that at the time this photograph was taken the house was intact so the rooms you can't recall were certainly in existence.'

'Which eliminates one possibility,' said Pat.

'What possibility is that?' Mina asked.

'In spite of what the agent said it could be possible that the rooms at the rear of the house were demolished for some reason before you moved in then rebuilt later, which would have accounted for you not remembering them.'

'Yes, it's very confusing,' Mina agreed. 'Now, if you turn the photo over ...'

Hodgkiss turned over the photo. On the back was written in pencil in faded copperplate script: *Mina and Me – Feb 1984.*

Hodgkiss nodded. 'Then we know that the house was intact in early 1984. When did your father ... disappear?'

'It was about then ...in early 1984 ... as far as I can tell. I think that's about the time Mum reported his disappearance ... around March, although I couldn't say for sure.'

Hodgkiss help up the photo. 'Would you mind if I make a copy of this?'

'A copy. Why?'

'Because I intend to approach my son-in-law, who is a Detective Inspector, and ask him to look into the matter. The photo might help. Is that all right with you?'

'Yes, I suppose so. Do you think he'll be able to find out anything about my father?'

Hodgkiss shrugged. 'Who knows. But one thing you can be sure of; I will see that he leaves no stone unturned to bring to light any information the police have on the matter, no matter how old. But first I'll need your mother and father's Christian names.'

'Mum's name was Maria and Dad's was Douglas. But please, Mr Hodgkiss ...'

'Edgar ... please.'

'Edgar ... I wouldn't want you to make a nuisance of yourself with your son-in-law for my sake.'

Pat smiled. 'Oh, don't worry about that, Mina. Donald's used to Edgar making a complete and utter nuisance of himself.'

Hodgkiss was about to protest but instead he reached for a blueberry friand.

*   *   *

'You're just making a bloody nuisance of yourself again, Dad. I mean this all happened more than twenty years ago. Right?'

Detective Inspector Donald Burke sat, his bulk wedged into the built-in pine breakfast nook in the kitchen of the family's bungalow in a quiet back street of suburban Lillimoor. His wife, Esme, Hodgkiss's daughter, had just set down on the table before him a generous breakfast of fried eggs, sausages, grilled tomato and mushrooms.

Donald picked up a bottle of tomato sauce, removed the cap and upended it over the plate then applied the heel of his palm vigourously to the bottom of the bottle.

Before Hodgkiss could comment on this procedure, as he had often in the past, Esme made a pre-emptive intervention: 'And don't you say a word, Dad. If Donald likes tomato sauce on his breakfast that's his affair.'

Hodgkiss, seated opposite Donald, nibbling a finger of

lightly buttered toast with a smear of marmalade, said: 'I am well aware of that, my dear. Nevertheless you can't blame me for being irritated when I am forced to witness this disgusting spectacle on several mornings each week.'

'And what disgusting spectacle might that be?' Donald inquired, putting down the bottle after he had persuaded it to discharge a large gout of red sauce onto the side of his plate.

'The spectacle of you spoiling perfectly good and not inexpensive food with your bizarre taste; that is what I find disgusting,' Hodgkiss replied heatedly.

Donald cut a sausage in two, skewered it with his fork and transferred it to his mouth.

'You criticise the way I eat my breakfast' he said through a mouthful of sausage, 'and in the same breath you demand that I waste half my busy day chasing up some twenty year old missing persons case. Now there's cheek for you.'

'Really, Donald, that is the most senseless *non sequiter*. What have your repulsive eating habits to do with my perfectly reasonable request for information that very likely is readily available with very little effort on your part?'

Donald ignored the question. 'Anyway, what's so special about this particular twenty-year-old missing person's case that makes it any different from the hundreds of other twenty-year-old missing person's cases on the books? And why are you so interested in it?'

'The matter was raised with me by a friend of Pat's, or rather by the daughter of a friend of Pat's; one Mina Cumberland.'

'That doesn't make it special,' Donald said, transferring half a tomato from the plate to his mouth.

'There are some rather unusual circumstances surrounding the disappearance,' Hodgkiss explained.

'What unusual circumstances?' Donald demanded.

'There is a suspicion that a serious crime was committed in the house around the time the fellow went missing.'

'Serious crime? What sort of serious crime?'

'Donald, if I knew all the details of the matter I would not be asking you to look into it. I would be investigating it myself. Are you going to assist me in this matter or are you not?'

Donald shook his head. 'Nope. I've got quite enough *proper* police work to keep me busy at present without getting involved in this frolic of yours which will almost certainly go nowhere and be a total waste of my time.'

'That's final, is it, Donald" You're not going to help? Is that what I should tell Pat?'

Donald put down his knife and fork with a clatter. 'Now, don't you come that sort of blackmail with me. I'd be quite prepared to have a look into it for Pat's sake if you had any-thing that might open up some new line of inquiry. Otherwise it'd almost certainly be a total waste of time.'

Hodgkiss raised an eyebrow. 'But I *do* have some fresh information on the matter that could well open up a new line of inquiry.'

'Well, why didn't you say so?'

'I would have if you hadn't kept interrupting.' He reached into his shirt pocket and took out the photo Mina had given him to copy. He put it down on the table facing Donald.

'The little girl aged about five is Wilhelmina Cumberland. It is she who Pat and I spoke to yesterday. She is now in her mid twenties. The lady holding her hand is, or was, her mother, Maria, now deceased. Mina was raised by an aunt.'

Donald picked up the photo. 'And the guy in the back-ground, who's he?'

'That we do not know, but Mina had always had the very

strong impression that he may have been the cause of her family's many problems. She has a strong recollection that her mother did not like the man … even that she feared him.'

'And when did this Wilhemina's father disappear?'

'In early 1984, probably around March.'

'And his name was …?

'Douglas Cumberland."

'Age?'

'I couldn't tell you, but I think we may assume he was in his thirties or forties when he disappeared.'

'And why is this Wilhemina so anxious to find out what happened to her father after all these years. Not just idle curiosity, I hope.'

'No, Donald. It is more than that. She became seriously concerned when recently she visited that house in the background of the photo, which is where the family lived at that time, and discovered that she had no recollection of the inside of the home with the exception of the kitchen and the bedroom where she slept with her mother, and a small entry hallway.'

'What!?' Donald exploded. 'You want me to undertake an investigation just because some girl can't remember every detail of the house where she lived as a kid.'

'She is *not* a girl,' Hodgkiss explained with determined reserve. 'She is a mature, sensible adult and having regard to all of the circumstances I am now strongly of the view that something bad, very bad, happened in that house which is the reason for this gap in her memory …. something traumatic which requires investigation.'

'And what does she say about it. Does she agree with your something-bad-happened theory.'

Hodgkiss decided an evasion was warranted. 'She has not ruled it out.'

Donald shook his head. 'No, Dad. That is simply not good enough. Unless you can come up with something a bit better than a girl's bad feeling I can't have anything to do with it. The boys in the missing person's branch would laugh at me.'

Hodgkiss snorted. 'Would they indeed. I fancy it would not be the first time that you were the object of mirth among your colleagues.'

Esme, fearing an outbreak of open hostilities, tried a reasonable intervention. 'Donald, perhaps you could just get your sergeant to dig out the old records and have a look just in case there's been some recent development.'

'My sergeant's got better things to do with his time than dig out old records on the off-chance.'

Hodgkiss snorted. 'Better things like preparing rosters for holidays, I suppose.'

Donald slid out of the breakfast nook. 'That's it,' he snapped. 'I'm off.' He pecked Esme on the cheek. 'I'll see you tonight.'

*　　*　　*

In her office at the Kanundda Council chambers building Jan Campbell-Jones swung her ergonomic chair through ninety degrees and stretched her long, elegant legs towards the centre of the room.

'It certainly is a most remarkable story, Hodgkiss. In fact I was tempted to use the word incredible,' she said into her tiny blue mobile phone.

'So you have doubts about it then, do you? You think she's making it up or she's hysterical?' Hodgkiss was slumped in the captain's chair in front of the computer in his bedroom at the front of the Burke's home.

'It could be a form of hysteria, I suppose, couldn't it?' said Jan. 'The mind plays funny tricks with some folk.'

'True, but she didn't strike me as the hysterical kind. But then I haven't had a great deal of experience in that field, except with Donald in his more excitable moments.'

'And what does Donald make of it? I assume you've tackled him about it.'

'Of course, and you will not be surprised to learn that he failed utterly to show the least glimmer of intelligent interest. He has refused point blank even to pull out the file on the old missing persons report to see if there'd been any action on it in recent times.'

Jan reached for a Styrofoam mug of black coffee on her side table. 'Can't say I blame him, Hodgkiss. One hopes that the boys in blue have more to do than chase up ancient events that may or may not have anything to do with criminality.'

'I have a distinct feeling that there is criminality somewhere at the bottom of this business, but I must confess that there is nothing much to support it other than instinct. Now, have you opened that email I just sent you?'

Jan swung back to her desk and touched the mouse attached to her computer. At once her screen came to life to display the inbox of her emails. She moved the cursor down to the most recent email and clicked.

'Yes, Hodgkiss. It has just arrived. Do you want me to look at it now?'

'If it's not too much trouble. I'm particularly interested to know what, if anything, you can tell me about the photo in the attachment.'

Jan clicked on the attachment and at once the photograph which Mina had given Hodgkiss appeared on the screen.

'Yes, I've got it. A photo of a woman holding a little girl by the hand. What about it?'

'It's no more than a shot in the dark, but do you recognise either of those people. The house is in Lambert Street, Rosbury. Number twenty. Actually it's on the market at the moment. That's how Mina Cumberland, the child in the photo, came to visit it; she saw it advertised for sale, recognised it as the place where she lived as a little girl and went to have a look.'

'Can't say that anything about the photo rings a bell with me. I can't place the house although I have friends in Lambert Street who I visit from time to time. And as for the woman and the little girl … I've never seen them before in my … but wait a moment. That fellow in the background leering at the woman over his shoulder. Now he looks more than a little familiar.'

Hodgkiss sat up. 'Familiar? You mean you recognise him? You know who he is?'

Jan hesitated. 'I wouldn't say that, but his face certainly reminds me of someone.'

'What? A friend? A relation? Someone you've known in the past?'

Jan shook her head. 'Be quiet for a moment, Hodgkiss. I'm trying to think. It's someone I see every day.' A short pause. 'Got it! It's Clive Fahey.'

'And who the hell is Clive Fahey when he's at home?'

'Clive Fahey is the deputy director of our health and environmental section.'

'Are you quite sure that's him? I mean that photo was taken more than twenty years ago. He'd have changed more than a little.'

'I realise that, Hodgkiss. Well, there's one way to find out, isn't there?'

'Show him the photo and ask him.'

'Obviously. Is there anything else you think I should ask him about?'

'You could ask him what he was doing there; what was his connection with the Cumberland family. You might also see if he can remember who took the photo. Is he at work today?'

'Yes, but very likely he'll be out of the office on some sort of inspection, or more likely having coffee somewhere with his mates. I'll go for a walk down to his floor, have a poke around and let you know.'

'I'll wait by the computer,' said Hodgkiss. 'Email me.'

Hodgkiss had not long to wait before an email arrived. *Email to ehodgkiss@ozemail.com.au*

Surprise, surprise! Our Mr Fahey was actually at his desk for a change. He informed he that he had been on his way out to an inspection somewhere but due to the fierce storm that has just blown up he decided to stay indoors until it has blown over. Can't say I blame him. It is very nasty outside right now as you must have noticed. Now, to the photo. He claims to know nothing about it or the persons in it. He denied vehemently that the leering man in the background was him. However I formed the strong impression that he was lying and that seeing that photo had brought back some very unwelcome recollections … something that seriously disturbed him for some reason. So, after I left his office I walked ten paces down the corridor, waited thirty seconds then returned on tiptoe, opened his door quietly and peeped in. He was engaged in a hushed, tense conversation with person or persons unknown. As soon as he saw me he put down his mobile phone and asked what did I want. I smiled sweetly and replied that it was not important

*and I would catch up with him some other time ... which
I will, make no mistake about it. I will keep an eye on
that particular gentleman. All in all his conduct was
very suspicious.*

   JC-J

   Email to jcampbell-jones@kanunddacouncil.com.au
*It would be of considerable interest to me if you could
discover just who he was speaking to in this hushed and
intense manner so soon after your encounter. I assume
that if he was using an official council mobile phone,
and since we know the precise time of his call, it would
not be difficult to find out what number he had called.
This could assist me in advancing my inquiries and in
possibly persuading Donald to treat the matter seriously.*

   EH

   Email to ehodgkiss@ozemail.com.au
*I will explore that possibility and keep you posted. But
it may take a day or two.*

   JC-J

       *   *   *

'Mal, it's Clive here. Guess what! That bitch Campbell-Jones
just came into my office with a photo of Maria Cumberland
and her brat ... with me in the background. Now, there's a
nasty blast from the past.'

'Where the hell did she get hold of that? It'd have to be
twenty years old, minimum.'

'And the rest. I reckon she's been dead more than twenty
years. And God knows where Jan got it from. Hold on a sec,
She's back. Yeah, Jan, Is there something else I can help you
with? Right. Catch up with you then. OK, she's gone. Said

there was something else she wanted to talk about but it'd keep. Now, where was I?'

'What'd you tell her about you being in the photo? We don't want anybody looking too closely at what happened way back then … in those days.'

'I wouldn't worry my head too much about that. Anyway, I denied it was even me in the photo and who's going to say it was?'

'Did it look like you?'

'Oh yeah, I suppose it did in a way. But I was only in the background. Anyway, it's no big deal. Listen, are we still on for coffee this morning?'

'Have you looked out your window? It's blowing a gale out there. I reckon it'll be a miracle if your emergency mob aren't called out to a few trees or power lines blown down. The way your council won't let anyone touch their bloody gum trees even when they're half dead it's a miracle we don't have more of the bloody things falling over.'

'No argument there. Then maybe I'll catch up with you this arvo if it blows over and if there's not too much cleaning up to do.'

*   *   *

'That was quite a blow yesterday. Was there any damage at your place?' Pat Strong was driving through the back streets of West Lillimoor, Hodgkiss beside her in the passenger's seat, a street map open in his lap.

Hodgkiss replied without looking up. 'No. Just the washing. Esme was out at the shops when it started raining and of course it all got soaked.'

'And you couldn't be bothered getting it in, I suppose,' said

Pat, turning to look disapproval.

'Nothing of the sort,' Hodgkiss replied. 'But it was all thoroughly wet through before I could rescue it.' He looked up from the map and scanned the street. 'Turn at the next corner and it's just there on the left.'

Pat slowed the big car, pushed down the indicator arm and turned.

'That must be it,' Hodgkiss announced pointing through the windscreen. 'Stop just here.'

'Thank you, Edgar. 'I'm quite sure I would never have worked out which house was for sale without your guidance,' said Pat, pulling to the kerb and stopping outside a white painted weatherboard bungalow with a large For Sale sign erected near the front gate.

On the nature strip a second, smaller sign, embedded in the grass on two metal prongs, announced – Now Open For Inspection.

Pat climbed out and looked around. 'Not a lot of other cars around so Mina probably hasn't arrived yet.' She glanced at her watch. 'But the inspection time has just started so she'll probably turn up soon. We might as well go straight in and have a look around before she gets here.'

Hodgkiss joined Pat and the two set off down the path, avoiding puddles which still lay in cracks in the uneven paving stones. At the front door the estate agent in charge of the Open Day, a well presented woman in her middle years, a badge bearing the name JENNY pinned to the lapel of a smart navy jacket, awaited them with an encouraging smile. She took their names and handed Hodgkiss a floor plan of the house. 'If you go out into the back yard please be careful, will you. A tree came down during that big blow yesterday and there's some damage to the lawn where it was uprooted.

There were emergency workers here half the afternoon and again this morning tidying up.'

'Yes, it was quite a blow,' said Pat chattily. 'Did it do any damage to the house itself?'

'Oh no,' said Jenny hastily. 'This house was very well built. It dates from the fifties and is completely original.'

Just then another car pulled up in the street outside and Mina climbed out. She saw Pat and Hodgkiss and waved.

Jenny also had spotted Mina. She waved and commented quietly to Hodgkiss and Pat: 'This lady is making her second inspection. She seems quite interested. Do you know her?'

'Just a friend of the family,' said Pat.

'Well, just look around and ask any questions you like,' said Jenny as Mina joined them in the small entry hall.

'I really had the horrors about coming here a second time,' said Mina as soon as Jenny had returned to her post at the front door to await the arrival of new prospects.

'Now the kitchen is through here,' Mina said, leading the way.

It was a large kitchen boasting all of the latest, most expensive whitegoods.

'Of course it was nothing like this when we lived here. There was just one noisy old fridge here and a gas stove over there in the corner. There was a bank of cupboards on the other wall and a sink and bench under the window. Now, our bedroom was through here.'

The room Mina led them into was no longer used as a bedroom. On the floor plan it was shown as a study and bookshelves lined two walls and a computer stood on a desk in front of the room's only window.

Mina crossed to the window that looked out onto the side of the house next door, a solid brick wall relieved only by one small window set with opaque glass.

'Not much of a view from my bedroom was it. It hasn't changed since I lived in here with Mum,' she said, then turned away.

Suddenly Hodgkiss and Pat became aware that Mina was sobbing quietly.

'Please, you'll have to excuse me,' she said. 'My memories of this room aren't very pleasant. I used to lie here at night sometimes with Mum and sometimes on my own listening to my father and other men in the kitchen drinking and laughing or more often arguing. I remember my father screaming at Mum through the door and she'd just lay there shaking. She was terrified of him, of all of them.' She smiled ruefully. 'Not the happiest of childhood memories. May we leave now, please? I don't want to go into any of those other rooms again; the ones I can't remember.'

Pat took Mina by the hand and led the way back through the kitchen to the entry hall.

'Perhaps we could just have a look around the back garden before we go,' Mina suggested. 'I don't think there are any bad memories out there.'

'The agent said there was a big tree uprooted by the storm in the back garden,' said Hodgkiss.

Mina led the way down a narrow crazy-paved side pathway to a back yard that sloped steeply towards the bottom of the garden where a paling fence, shrunken and weathered grey with age, divided the yard from two houses at the rear.

Near the fence was an area of broken grass and pitted soil sprinkled liberally with sawdust.

Pat commented. 'Looks like the emergency service people have been busy with their chain saws cutting up the tree that blew over.'

Mina paused, frowning. 'I don't remember any big trees in the back yard,' she said. Then she shrugged. 'But I wouldn't, would I? I don't even remember most of the house.'

Hodgkiss walked down to inspect the area of damaged grass, the others followed.

'Nasty blow yesterday,' said a man's voice nearby.

Hodgkiss looked up to see the head and shoulders of an elderly red-headed man over the back fence.

'Yes,' said Hodgkiss. 'Did you see it fall … the tree?' he asked indicating the broken ground.

The man nodded. 'Yes, I was looking out of my sunroom window at the time.' He nodded towards the house behind him. 'First a couple of little branches blew off then the whole thing just slowly keeled over.' He raised then lowered his forearm slowly in imitation of the falling tree.

He paused then added. 'I remember the day they planted that tree. Must have been … oh, twenty years ago. I remember because I thought at the time that it might grow too high and take the sun off my backyard.'

'You've got a pretty good memory,' said Hodgkiss.

The man nodded. 'Yeah. But that wasn't the only reason I remembered it. There were others.'

Hodgkiss looked up sharply. 'Oh. And what were they?'

'Because of the goings-on over there at the time.'

'The going's-on?'

'Yeah. There were some strange going's-on over there the night they planted the tree and again yesterday after the blow.'

'They planted the tree at night? That was a bit strange, wasn't it?'

The man nodded. 'Yes. That's one of the reasons I remember it. I didn't actually see them plant it although I remember seeing people with torches moving around that night in the dark; very odd I thought. Then, lo and behold, the next morning when I came out there it was. Of course it wasn't very tall then; only about that high.'

The man reached over the fence to indicate a height of about a metre.

'And what about the goings on yesterday … after the storm … after it was blown over. What was that about?'

The man frowned. 'It was a bit odd too. As soon as the tree came down I rang the emergency service people because I know that no one's living in the house right now. Anyway, before the emergency service people turned up another fellow arrived, I think he was from the council, and when the emergency services fellows turned up he told them to buzz off and that council would look after it. And sure enough about half an hour later a crew from the council came along and cut it up and took it away. It took them a while, too. They were here until well after dark tidying up.'

Hodgkiss asked: 'This fellow who told the emergency services people to go away; do you know who he was?'

The man shook his head. 'No. Never seen him before so far as I can remember. But I wouldn't, would I? I have as little to do with the council as I can manage.'

'Do you think you'd recognise him if you saw him again.'

The man frowned. 'Yes. I think so.'

'And the other workmen who came and cut up the tree and took it away; how do you know they were from council?'

'Because a couple of them were wearing gear with the council's logo on it. Outdoors staff they're called, I think.'

'And what time do you think they finished work here?'

'Couldn't tell you exactly, but it was well after dark. I was out in my yard here a lot of the time doing my own clearing up. I had leaves and twigs everywhere.'

The man turned to go away but hesitated then turned back. 'There'd been a history of trouble with that house you know... although to be fair I suppose you could say it was more trouble with the council ... as usual.'

'Oh, what sort of trouble was that?'

'Well, it was to do with the lie of the land. Years ago council did some work on the drainage in the next street, Lambert Street where that house faces, and what happened after that was that whenever it rained really hard the stormwater used to flood straight through there and into my place and the place next door. It was like a torrent at times.'

'And how long ago was that?'

The man shrugged. It all happened around the same time; maybe twenty years ago.'

'You mean about the time they planted the tree,' Hodgkiss said indicating the broken soil.

'Yeah. It'd've been about then I suppose.'

'And did it flood just the one time or on several occasions?'

'Oh several times. As I recall, that year we had steady rain for about a week and it just flooded and flooded. A real nuisance it was. My whole backyard was under water for days and I was damned lucky it didn't come right through my house. Council workers built a little levee with sandbags next door to stop the water from going into their place because most of the water ran in that direction.'

Hodgkiss nodded. 'And what about the people who were living here, at this property; what did they do about the flooding?'

'Oh there were people from council down there all the time poking around in the yard and under the house. At one point the flooding was so bad that the back part of that house was in danger of being undermined and washed away, or so

I heard from one of the council workmen.'

'Is that so! Thank you very much. You have been very helpful.'

The man added hastily. 'But if you're thinking of buying the place there's no need to worry about it now. That drainage problem was fixed up years ago. It hasn't flooded since then. They changed all the drainage arrangements further up the road near the highway so that all the water gets carried away properly underground … like they should have done in the first place.'

Hodgkiss turned to indicate a wooden garage standing nearby at the rear of the house.

'I suppose the water used to run through the garage too when it flooded.'

The man nodded. 'Yes. It poured through there … it went through everywhere. But like I said; there's nothing wrong with the drainage these days. There's absolutely nothing to worry about if you're thinking of buying the place.'

The man waved a cheery goodbye and retreated towards his back door.

Hodgkiss turned to Pat and Mina who had been standing close behind him. 'Did you hear all that?'

Mina nodded. 'I don't remember a thing about the flooding or the tree being planted. But of course I wouldn't, would I? I was only very small at the time.'

They followed as Hodgkiss headed towards the garage.

'It looks like it's fitted with one of those automatic electric doors,' said Pat. 'Do you want me to go back and see if Jenny has the remote to open it?'

'Wait a moment,' said Hodgkiss. 'That may not be necessary. That side door might be open.'

He followed a small cement path to a battered-looking wooden door in the side wall which proved to be unlooked.

He pulled the door open and looked in. The others crowded behind him.

'Anything in there?' Pat asked.

Hodgkiss stepped in and the others followed.

The contents of the garage appeared unexceptional. Crudely made shelves were attached precariously to both long walls and on the shelves stood a variety of old jars containing nails and screws, old paint cans and dried paint brushes sitting in jars whose contents had long since evaporated.

A workbench had been built against the rear wall and on the wall above the bench was a board displaying the painted outline of a number of tools none of which hung in its designated place.

A painter's dropsheet, stained with a variety of pastel colours, hung down over the front of the bench.

Hodgkiss looked about for a second time then headed for the side door.

At the door he hesitated and Pat, who had been following closely, collided with him.

'What is it, Hodgkiss?' she asked.

'I was just wondering ... excuse me.'

He brushed past Pat and headed back towards the workbench. He stopped and reached for the painter's dropsheet.

With an energetic tug Hodgkiss pulled it away to reveal parts of what were unmistakably parts of a human skeleton. Fresh wet earth still adhered to many of the bones.

Pat and Mina stood silently behind him, shocked.

He turned to Mina. 'Your father, I fear.'

*   *   *

'Mal. They've found Douglas.'

'Bloody hell! How do you know that, Clive?'

'I went back to the place this morning pretending I wanted to make an inspection. I just wanted to keep an eye on things and just as well, too, because I saw a group of people, an old guy and two women, go into the garage and come hurrying out minutes later, one of them – the old guy — was ringing on his mobile. I cleared out before they arrived back in the house and parked down the end of the street to see what happened and sure enough the cops and an ambulance turned up there within minutes. It's a bloody good thing I hot-footed it over there as soon as my mate in the emergency services tipped me off about that tree coming down. If I hadn't it would have been the emergency service guys instead of us who found Doug in that hole.'

'Well, it hasn't made much difference, has it? It's out in the open now. Jees, Clive, I said we should've moved him out last night when we had the chance.'

'Hindsight's a wonderful thing, Mal. But it would have been risky with those emergency services guys still hanging around and the old bloke from the house behind looking over the fence every few minutes. And that's another thing. The old bloke with a beard who went into the garage and rang the cops ... he's a friend of the Campbell-Jones woman.'

'Yeah? How d'you know that?'

'Because I've seen him with her around the building. His name's Hodgkiss. I wonder how he fits into this business, if at all.'

'What if he does? Is it a problem?'

'Nah. Probably not. But it might be worthwhile keeping an eye on things. Another thing, that Hodgkiss fellow spent a lot of time talking to the old guy over the back fence before he went into the garage. God knows what he told him.'

'What could he tell him that'd matter? What does he know?'

'Well, he knows that we were there 'til all hours in the dark last night.'

'Yeah. But he couldn't have actually seen anything. Could he? And do you think he could recognise any of us if he saw us again?'

'Nah. Probably not. It was dark most of the time. But the whole situation bears watching.' He paused. 'I suppose the cops'll be all over that house like a rash now … and the back yard too. It'd be just our luck if after all these years the cops actually find it.'

'No way. We went over that place with a fine tooth comb, and more than once. Every inch. There's no doubt in the wide world that bloody Doug held out on us and hid it, but sure as hell he never hid it there.'

'No. I guess not. But it's gotta be somewhere.'

'Yeah. But where?'

*   *   *

'And what makes you think those bones belong to that missing guy you told me about … what's-his-name Cummerbund?'

Donald was seated at the round redwood table on the back deck, a can of beer in one hand.

Hodgkiss, seated opposite, shook his head in exasperation. 'Oh, for heaven's sake, use your common sense, Donald. And the fellow's name was Cumberland … Douglas Cumberland. Now, if you had initiated inquiries when I first raised the matter …'

'We'd have been no further ahead. For a start we haven't got a clue if you're right or not about who those bones belong to. Could be anyone, so what makes you so sure it's this Cumberland fellow?'

'It's the timing. He disappeared at exactly the time that tree was planted.'

'And what tree might this be? I don't know anything about a tree.'

'The tree he was buried under ... the tree that was blown over in that big storm yesterday. What must have happened is that the people who buried him there somehow heard about it being blown over and went back ASAP to make sure that he was still resting in peace where they'd put him twenty years earlier.'

'Oh, Dad, spare me. That's pure guess work. Admit it.'

'Nothing of the sort. A fellow who lives in the house behind told me that the regular emergency workers who usually attend to the problems created by fallen trees were sent away by someone from council and that a group of council workers took over and were still there until after dark.

'OK! So it was council staff who removed the blown-down tree. So what?'

'So why were the regular emergency workers sent away? Tell me that. It was because someone from council knew what was under that tree, and when that someone arrived he discovered that when the tree came down the odd bone or two had come to the surface for any intending house purchaser to discover during the course of an inspection.

'So obviously something had to be done.

'What he did was to remove the visible bones from the ground and hide them in the garage.

'Then he contacted some of his mates among the council workers to come and deal with the tree. No doubt he intended to come back as soon as the coast was clear and remove

Cumberland from the garage to a second, more private and permanent resting place.'

'Rubbish. Absolute guesswork. So can you put a name to this someone; this mysterious undertaker engaged in unauthorised burials?'

'There are one or two candidates for the position but more datum is required before I could put a name to him with any certainty.'

Donald scoffed. 'Yeah! I thought that might be the case. And how do you know it's Cumberland who was buried under that tree?'

'It has to be. I've told you once; his disappearance coincides with the planting of the tree.'

'And how do you know that? Were you there at the time?'

Hodgkiss remained unruffled. 'No. But I've spoken to someone who was.'

'Oh. And who might that be?'

'I don't know the fellow's name but he lives in the property directly behind the Cumberland's old home.'

'And what else did this mystery informant tell you?'

'He told me that he had seen men skulking in the back yard of that house the night the tree was planted and he saw men skulking in the back yard again last night after it was blown down.'

Donald shook his head in disbelief. 'And do you mean to tell me that although there was a break of twenty years between these two skulking events he still remembers it all as if it was yesterday. Remarkable.'

'I do not agree. I don't think it is at all remarkable. But the point is; what do you intend to do about it?'

'I intend to conduct a routine police investigation into the discovery of those bones ... a rational, routine investigation.

For a start we don't even know for sure that they're human bones or that they were actually buried under where that tree stood. We'll have to wait for the results of an examination of the earth that was found on them before we know for sure that's where they were buried.

'Then, if it turns out that he *was* buried there, assuming the bones were those of a male person, then we can begin the task of identifying him. And that may not be so simple after all this time.'

'Nonsense, Donald. That will be the easy part. Just compare the DNA of the bones with Mina's DNA. That will confirm his identity.'

'Maybe, maybe not. And even if it does that'll be only the start. The cause of death will have to be established, and that's not always so easy after such a long time and particularly when there are bits missing.'

Hodgkiss nodded, smiling wanly. 'I suspect that it will not prove too difficult on this occasion.'

'Oh, And why do you say that?'

'Because he was an unpleasant, violent man and probably he died an unpleasant and violent death. I would say that damage would appear on some bones, particularly the skull, which, I noticed, was among the bones in the garage.'

'You know all about him then, do you, although he's been dead for twenty years?' Donald asked sarcastically, taking a long suck from his beer.

'I have heard enough about him and about his associates to know that he was a bad, violent man who treated his family with contempt. But I see no point in prolonging this conversation. You will proceed in your usual pedestrian manner and probably in due course will arrive at some conclusion ... very likely erroneous. Meanwhile I will pursue my own inquiries into the matter and pass on any information I glean, which, very likely, you will choose to ignore as you have so often in the past ... to your detriment.'

Hodgkiss pushed back his bench seat and headed for the sliding door to the family room. At the door he turned. 'I trust you will not be driving back to the station after consuming a whole can of beer.'

Without waiting for a response Hodgkiss headed back to his bedroom where he settled in front of the computer and opened the email.

Almost at once a sharp electronic beep announced the arrival of an email. He opened the inbox to discover a message from Jan Campbell-Jones

Email to ehodgkiss@ozemail.com.au

Well, I managed to trace the number of that phone call Fahey was making when I doubled back to his office yesterday. It was 0410 235 109. I could possibly, through my unofficial contacts, discover whose number that is, but I'm sure Donald could find out much more quickly and legally if you could prevail upon him to oblige.

JC-J

Email to jcampbell-jones@kanunddacouncil.com.au

Normally I would hold out little hope that we would, as you put it, oblige. However, recent events of which you may not yet be aware should encourage him to apply himself more diligently to the matter.

Yesterday Pat, Mina Cumberland and I made an open day inspection of that premises. We had the unfortunate experience of discovering part of a skeleton concealed in the garage. There is little doubt that it is the remains of Mina's father who disappeared about the time a tree under which the bones were discovered, was planted.

The tree was blown down in yesterday's storm and some bones exposed, removed and hidden in the garage on the property by person or persons unknown. Donald, however, is not persuaded. Since this Clive Fahey person is involved in the matter it seems that in the circumstances the person he was talking to in furtive tones immediately after you had shown him the photo demonstrating his connection with the Cumberland family, also is involved. Not a great leap into the unknown although it is unlikely that Donald will see the simple logic of it. However, I can but try. I will approach him now before he leaves for the police station, with a request to trace the number, and keep you posted.

Oh, and there was one other matter of interest. Do you have any record of serious flooding at that property about twenty years ago; flooding caused by faulty drainage in the area? I ask this because it is about that time that this whole business has its genesis. Very likely there is some connection.

EH

Hodgkiss wrote down the phone number given in Jan's message, closed the email and returned hurriedly to the back deck. He sat down again and placed the paper with the phone number down on the table.

'And what's that?' Donald asked.

'It is the phone number of someone who I think will prove to be involved in some criminal way with that skeleton.'

Donald's eyebrows rose sharply. 'Really. And where did you get that number?'

'Does that matter? Surely what matters is that we discover ...'

'It may not matter to you, but it sure matters to me. You

just lob out here with a number written down on a scrap of paper, you won't say how it might be connected to this business and you won't even say who gave it to you, then you expect me to trace it for you. Well, Dad, it doesn't work that way. Now, who gave you the number and what has this person got to do with my investigation? You tell me that and then I'll decide if it's worth making the inquiries. Savvy?'

Hodgkiss sighed. 'Very well, Donald. Seeing that it would take me an ordinately long time to discover the necessary information through my own resources I suppose I have no choice but to rely on you. The phone number was provided to me by Jan Campbell-Jones who, I am sure you will agree, is a most credible and reliable person.'

'And why's it so important to find out whose number it is?'

'Because that is the number dialed by the creepy-looking man in that photo I showed you, shortly after Jan had con-fronted him with the photo.'

'So now you know who it is in that photo?'

'That's what I just said, Donald, although the man denied it is him.'

'And who is this man who denies it's him?'

'His name is Clive Fahey. Jan recognised him when I emailed the photo to her. She showed it to him and although he denied it, Jan is quite sure, judging from his reaction, that he was lying and she is convinced that it *is* him. Then after she left his office she let a few seconds go by then doubled back, opened the door and sure enough there he was engaged in a guilty, whispered conversation with whoever answers this phone number.'

Donald shook his head. 'It's all pretty thin, Dad.'

'You mean you won't do it?'

'I didn't say that. I just said it was pretty thin and I don't really see what we'll learn by finding out who this Fahey fellow was ringing. What do we know about Fahey and his involvement with Mina Cumberland and her family?'

'I do not have a great deal of information on that matter at the moment, Donald, but I am making certain inquiries that may well throw some light on it.'

'Oh are you? Certain inquiries eh?! I don't suppose you'd like to tell me what these certain inquiries are?'

'There is no reason why I shouldn't. I have asked Jan to look into the history of that property. If her inquiries reveal the sort of information I anticipate, they will throw some light on events that took place there at that time.'

'That time? What time is that?'

'Really, Donald, when you ask questions like that it seems to me that you haven't been taking a scrap of notice of anything I've been telling you. The important time in this matter is twenty years ago; the period when all of these events took place.'

'When this Cumberland fellow is supposed to have disappeared, you mean?'

'Of course. What did you think? But his disappearance was not the only significant event in relation to that property twenty years ago. At almost exactly the same time there was a series of serious of floods through the Cumberland place and two properties at the rear. This flooding was caused by the poor design of a new drainage system which council installed further up the road from where the Cumberland's lived.'

'And you reckon the flooding had something to do with this Cumberland guy's disappearance. You reckon he was washed away perhaps?'

'Donald. This is no laughing matter. Now, I believe that our joint interests will be best served by you applying your resources to the missing persons file, ascertaining the identity and criminal record of the person who answers that phone number and also having a look to see if Clive Fahey is, as they say, known to police.'

'So you reckon he might be involved in Cumberland's disappearance?'

Hodgkiss shrugged. 'Really, Donald, I've no idea, but some light may be thrown on that question when we have the identity and antecedents of the person with whom he spoke during that phone call. Wouldn't you agree?'

Donald shrugged and finished his beer with a single gulp. 'Let's just wait and see.'

'I trust you have put in motion a request for the old papers relating to the missing persons report on Cumberland.'

'They should be on my desk when I get back to the office.'

Hodgkiss glanced at the empty beer can.

'If you ask Esme I'm sure she could find time to drive you to the station rather than have you drive yourself there in an intoxicated state.'

'Dad,' Donald exploded. 'I've had one can of beer. I wouldn't even register on the breathalyzer.'

Hodgkiss shook his head ruefully and rose. He was headed for the kitchen when the cordless phone in the hall rang. He scooped up the handset as he passed.

'Yes, what is it?' he snapped.

In her office Jan Campbell-Jones shook her head. 'I know someone who would benefit considerably from a few lessons in basic telephone manners.'

'Donald has an unfortunate knack of infuriating me,' Hodgkiss offered by way of an apology. 'He has such an unforgivably lackadaisical approach to every investigation he undertakes. He fails to recognise the obvious when it is presented to him on a plate.'

'Yes, so I've heard you tell him on more than one occasion. Well, I have some more information which you may think worth presenting to Donald on a plate to see if he treats it lackadaisically.'

'Just a moment then. You've caught me half way down the hall.' Hodgkiss turned and headed quickly for his bedroom where he settled on the end of his bed, a pad and pencil at the ready. 'Very well. Now what have we got.'

'It's about that flooding you mentioned. My P.A. Jenny Cope has dug up a huge old file that goes into great detail about it. And it contains some very, very interesting information; material which I would say has a direct bearing on your problem.'

Hodgkiss nodded vigourously. 'Excellent.'

'Well, it all started in 1983 with our engineering department's plans for the new drainage system near the intersection of the Northern Highway and Lambert Street which is where your friend used to live as a little girl.

'Drainage in the area had been a problem for years. There had been a series of complaints from residents on the low side of Lambert Street about flooding on their properties.

'The new arrangement was meant to overcome all of that. And so it did except in cases of very heavy rainfall.

'Then in February and March 1984 there was some unusually heavy rain and the new drainage, which had only been completed the previous July, had its first real test.'

'And it failed?!'

'In a big way. Several houses, including number twenty, where the Cumberlands lived at the time, were flooded several times in a matter of days.

'There are numerous complaints on record from a Mrs

Maria Cumberland who rang on at least seven occasions over that period. All her calls were logged as were calls from two other householders who lived at the rear of the Cumberland's home.'

'Do you have the names of these other complainants?'

'I do. Do you have a pen handy? The names were Adrian Gilbert and James Hardaker.'

'Thank you, Jan. Now, do you have an exact date for these complaints?'

'I certainly do. I have the file in front of me as we speak. Let me see now. Most of the letters of complaint and numerous phone calls cover a period between February 28 and March seventeen so no doubt that was the period of the worst flooding.

'Now, Hodgkiss, I have one other snippet that I think you'll find of more than passing interest. You remember Roger Ives of course.'

'How could I forget him. Do you mean to tell me that he's involved in this?'

'Up to his tricky little neck. He was a junior officer in the outdoor maintenance section at the time and his name appears on the file at several points. In fact he was the officer appointed to liaise with the people who had complained with a view to getting feed back from them on how our efforts to solve the problem were working.'

'Not a very good choice for the job I'd say if the object of the exercise was to keep the complainants fully informed and happy with progress.'

'No. And it's apparent from the files that he did anything *but* keep them fully informed and happy.

'In fact it is pretty plain from some of the comments from Mrs Cumberland that Ives did everything he could to scare her out of her wits.

'On the file I found a copy of one letter to her which hadn't been stamped with a signature so I can't be sure if it was actually posted or not, but in it Ives claimed that the flooding had been so strong and the damage to her house so severe that the house might have to be condemned and demolished.

'Now, there is a record of a phone call from Mrs Cumberland in which she claims that someone from council had suggested that her house had become unsafe. No doubt that was Ives at work. He must have put the fear of God into the poor woman.'

'And were there any grounds for that suggestion?'

'No, none whatsoever. In fact I found a report from one of our engineers who inspected the property after Mrs Cumberland complained about what she had been told about the house being unsafe, and he found that there was no sug-gestion of any structural damage, but unfortunately there's nothing to show that this advice was ever passed on to the Cumberlands.'

Hodgkiss nodded. 'Makes one wonder what game Ives was playing at. He could have had something really unpleas-ant in store for the Cumberlands, especially having regard to what we know now about his criminal proclivities.'

'Heaven alone knows what he had in mind. But I'm still looking into it and I think it highly likely that more informa-tion will come to light. If so I'll keep you posted. By the way, has Donald come up with anything of interest?'

'No, but I think he'll trace that number you gave me and he assured me that he will look at the old missing persons file, but I'm not holding my breath. He moves at glacial pace. Be in touch when I have anything of interest.'

*   *   *

Hodgkiss had just settled down to watch the six o'clock news when he heard Donald's unmarked police car turn in at the driveway. Five minutes later Donald appeared at the family room door, can of beer in hand.

Hodgkiss looked pointedly at the can then remarked: 'Honestly Donald, I think you are at risk of becoming an alcoholic. Don't you think it would be a good idea to moderate your intake?'

'An alcoholic!' Donald exploded. 'On two or three cans a day. You're out of your mind, Dad. An alcoholic is a person who can't do without it.'

'That's perfectly true, Donald. So do you think you could go without beer for, say, a week? I'd be prepared to stake one hundred dollars that you couldn't. What do you say?'

'I say you're talking a lot of nonsense. Now do you want to hear what I've found out about your missing person, Douglas Cumberland?'

Hodgkiss reached for the TV remote and pressed the Mute button. 'If it's not too much trouble.'

Donald took a scrap of paper from his shirt pocket. 'The missing person's report was made by Mrs Wilhemina Cumberland who called in person at the Crestwood police station on March 20, 1984 at 11.08 a.m. She told the sergeant that she had not seen her husband since 8 p.m. on March 18. She said that when she last saw him he was in the company of two associates at their address at twenty Lambert Street.'

Hodgkiss cut in. 'Did she give the name of these associates?'

'Hold your horses, Dad. I was just coming to that. Their names were Malcolm Corbett and Roger Ives.'

Hodgkiss nodded grimly. 'Yes, and we know all about Mr Ives, don't we. I assume he is still safely tucked away in gaol.'

Donald nodded. 'He is indeed. I checked on that, and no doubt I'll be paying him a visit in the very near future; tomorrow in fact.' He glanced down at the paper again. 'Now, about that phone number Jan gave you to check out. Guess who that belongs to?'

Hodgkiss shook his head. 'Please, Donald, I am in no mood for silly guessing games, but no doubt it will turn out to be a criminal associate of Douglas Cumberland and possibly also of Roger Ives.'

Donald nodded. 'Yeah, of course. But there's more to it than that. The phone belongs to Malcolm Corbett, one of the people Mina Cumberland named as an associate of her husband.'

'Well, that's hardly surprising, is it? What we need to find out is exactly what form of criminality was involved in the relationship between these people?'

'I think you could say they were very catholic in their criminal tastes. Ives, as we know, was a long term employee of the Kanundda Council, and ...'

'Yes, I am already aware of his role in attempting to frighten Mrs Cumberland out of her home with stories about the house being seriously damaged due to the effects of flooding.'

'I suppose Jan told you about that, eh? But that wasn't all he was up to. According to statement made by Malcolm Corbett, Ives was also the main source of information that helped them to carry out a number of successful jewellery robberies. Ives was in a position to give them details of certain premises that helped them plan their robberies.'

Hodgkiss nodded. 'I suppose he had access to floor plans and electrical wiring diagrams and that kind of thing. But that would have been of limited use.'

'No doubt, but he was also active in giving out information about future zoning arrangements to various folk with enough money to take advantage of the situations.'

'And who told you that?'

'Corbett told me. I've just had a long conversation with him. He's a very bitter man. He has been out of gaol for only a little under two years. He'd served a longish sentence for a jewellery robbery, but what's made him really sour is that he's convinced that somehow Ives or Cumberland or both of them conspired to dud him out of the proceeds of an even bigger job they'd done many years ago at a leading jewellery store in the city.'

'When was that, do you know?'

'Donald consulted his piece of paper. 'Yes. That was in early March 1984. According to Corbett they took the stuff back to Cumberland's place and hid it there in case the police came looking for Corbett and the stolen jewellery. Corbett was well known as a jewel thief and when this burglary was carried out he was the first person the police thought of because it was his *modus operandi* used to get into the shop.

'Anyway, the police knew that Cumberland was an associate of Corbett and when they called at Cumberland's place a few days later they questioned Corbett and Cumberland who, not surprisingly, pleaded complete ignorance of the whole business. The police searched the house from top to bottom but found nothing.

'Corbett swore to me that the stolen jewels were definitely somewhere around the house at the time because after the police had gone Ives went out and came back just minutes later with the jewels all wrapped up in a kind of oil skin bag.

'Corbett says he examined them at the time and he swears they were all there and I can tell you, Dad, because

I've checked, that to this day none of those stolen jewels have ever been recovered. Corbett also swore that he never found out where Ives had hidden them before the police called, although it was obviously somewhere very close by because of the speed with which Ives recovered them after the police had left.'

'And do you know exactly what was stolen?'

'Yes. I've got a complete list. Do you want it?'

'That will not be necessary, thank you, Donald. Just a general indication.'

'Well, for a start it wasn't jewellery in the form of rings or brooches or necklaces, or things like that. All they took in that robbery was precious stones; diamonds, emeralds, rubies … nothing but the biggest and the best. That particular jeweller was well-known in the trade for keeping only the very best gems in stock.'

Hodgkiss stroked his short, well-trimmed beard. 'I see. Small. Portable. Easily concealed. Very professional. Now, what do you have about Clive Fahey, the fellow at Kanundda Council who Jan caught ringing Corbett.'

Donald nodded. 'Oh yes. He's on record too. But a long time ago. According to Corbett, Fahey and Ives worked together in the same section at Kanundda Council and they were in on various scams involving under-the-counter land deals to help out some of their local estate agent and developer mates. Mostly small time stuff, or so Corbett said.

'But he told me one thing with a bearing on this business; he reckons that Fahey arranged for the purchase of Mrs Cumberland's house on behalf of Ives after Cumberland had disappeared and his wife and child had moved out, which was very soon after she'd made the missing person report.

'Corbett said that Fahey bought the place very cheaply

because Mrs Cumberland was under the impression it was just about falling down because it had been flooded out a few times and was seriously undermined.'

Hodgkiss nodded. 'That was because Ives lied to her about it. Jan has found an engineer's report saying there was nothing wrong with the house. What scum those people are to take advantage of that poor woman like that. I think I should contact Jan and see if she can find out any more about Fahey now that we know of his connection with Corbett, Ives and Cumberland. Do you have any objection to that, Donald?'

'Would it make any difference if I did?'

Hodgkiss smiled. 'No. Not a scrap. Also with or without your leave I will pass this information on to Pat who is still concerned with her friend Mina's condition.'

*   *   *

'Clive, I thought you should know,' said Malcolm Corbett. 'I've just had a long talk to one of the local boys in blue I know quite well. Apparently they're pretty sure that it is Doug they found in the garage although they couldn't know yet for certain.'

Clive Fahey nodded. 'I expect they'll do a DNA test using Maria's girl and that'll clinch it, eh? Shouldn't take them too long. But even so, what'll that prove?'

'Nothing much I suppose, but one thing's for sure; in a day or two the coppers'll be all over that old missing person's case. Now, you've always been square with me, so I'm just letting you know that I've been talking to them because I've always reckoned that you didn't have anything to do with Doug's disappearing. I always thought that Ives was behind it ... particularly now that we know he's got no conscientious objection to killing folk.'

'That's true enough. And thanks for not thinking the worst of me. If the coppers want to talk to me I've got nothing to hide … not about Doug anyway.'

'No, I didn't think so. I can remember how Roger lost it completely the night Doug went out to fetch the jewels and came back and told us that they'd disappeared. I must say I wouldn't have believed him either except I knew him better than Roger did, and I knew he wouldn't try to hold out on us. But Roger … well, he was another matter, wasn't he. He always had a pretty short fuse. When I heard from Maria that Doug had disappeared I thought then that maybe … you know.'

'Personally I don't think there's any doubt about it. It had to be Roger that did for him.'

'Well. Time will tell. I wonder what really happened to all those jewels. They were worth a bloody fortune you know, and they'd be worth an even bigger fortune these days I guess.'

'Yeah. They've gotta be somewhere. The ground just didn't open up and swallow them.'

'I suppose they'll turn up somewhere one day, but it won't do us a lot of good, eh?'

*　　　*　　　*

Pat edged the Mercedes into the kerb outside the well-kept wooden bungalow, stopped and pulled on the handbrake gently.

'So how did you find out the fellow's name?' she asked.

'From Jan. It was in some old papers about the floods that went through Mina's parents' property. Adrian Gilbert and one of his neighbours, a fellow called James Hardaker, they were also adversely affected.'

'"Adversely affected!" You've been reading too many official reports, Hodgkiss.'

'Nonsense. It says what I mean to say; the effect of the flooding had an adverse effect on their property. How would you describe it?'

'Never mind,' said Pat, climbing out of the car and walking around to join Hodgkiss on the nature strip.

A man whom Hodgkiss recognised as the man he had spoken to over the back fence of Mina Cumberland's childhood home, was standing at the front gate of the property.

Hodgkiss stepped forward, hand outstretched. 'Adrian Gilbert, is it? I'm Edgar Hodgkiss and this is a friend of mine, Pat Strong.'

Gilbert nodded a greeting and pulled the gate open. 'Come in,' he muttered.

Gilbert's wife, introduced as Edna, had set out a morning tea on the front veranda.

When they were settled Gilbert said: 'Since you rang I've been thinking about it and I'd say that I've already told you just about everything I can remember about what happened back then, when we had those floods ... and about the time that they planted that tree that was blown down the other day.

'That flooding was a damned nuisance. Parts of our back fence adjoining the Cumberland's place was completely washed down. We had mud all through the garage and we were just jolly lucky that it didn't come right through the house.'

'You mentioned that council put sandbags next door to stop it going into their house,' said Hodgkiss.

Gilbert nodded. 'That's right. I helped fill the bags. Some of the time the flooding next door was even worse than here.'

'And was their back fence washed down too.'

'Yes it was, flattened in parts, the same as ours. I remember that because James Hardaker and I got together to get a quote to replace the lot of it.'

'And do the Hardakers still live next door?'

'Oh no. They left years ago. I think they'd had it, what with the flooding and everything.'

'So they sold up and moved away? Do you know where they went?'

Mrs Gilbert answered. 'Yes. I kept in touch with Lesley, Jim's wife. They moved to a very nice unit on the waterfront down on the Northern Beaches somewhere. Lesley said she'd always wanted to go somewhere where she had a water view.'

Gilbert chuckled. 'I told her that I thought she must have had enough of a water view from her back door.'

'How soon after the flooding did the Hardakers move?' Hodgkiss asked.

'Not long at all,' said Gilbert. He turned to his wife. 'What would you say, Edna … two months would it've been?'

Edna nodded. 'Maybe three. No more. As soon as we'd fixed the back fence the For Sale sign went up next door and they were gone not long after. They didn't hang about.'

Hodgkiss nodded. 'I see. I don't suppose you have their present address, do you?'

'Jim died not long after they moved but Lesley stayed on in the unit for quite a few years after that, but she's in a home now.'

'Do you have her address?'

'Yes. I still send her a card at Christmas time, but I haven't had one back for the past few years. I know she's still alive because I hear from her daughter now and then, but Lesley … well, she's away with Pixies a lot of the time, or so her daughter told me.'

Hodgkiss nodded. 'Nevertheless I think I might want to pay her a visit.'

Karen put down her mug and rose. 'If you wait just a moment I'll get her address for you.'

As they were leaving Hodgkiss paused with a hand on the handle of the car's door.

'What is it, Hodgkiss? Forget something?' Pat asked.

'I wonder if they're home next door,' said Hodgkiss turning to look at the adjacent property. 'The Hardaker's place.'

'But they left years ago. Mr Gilbert just told us that,' Pat objected.

'I know that, Pat,' said Hodgkiss peevishly. 'I'm not yet totally senile. I just thought it might be worthwhile speaking to the neighbours, particularly if they're the people who bought the house from the Hardakers.'

Pat shrugged and followed as Hodgkiss headed for the front gate of the neighbouring home.

A trim, smartly dressed woman in her fifties opened the door to Hodgkiss's aggressive knocking. 'Yes, what is it?' she demanded. 'I was just on my way out.'

Hodgkiss smiled and tried a conciliatory approach. 'We were wondering if it was you who bought this property from the Hardakers when it was for sale about twenty years ago.'

The woman frowned. 'Yes, I think that's the name of the people we bought it from. Why do you want to know? We're not thinking of selling or anything.'

Hodgkiss shook his head, still smiling. 'No, and we're not looking to buy. We're just trying to trace where the Hardakers went to live after they left here.'

The woman shook her head. 'Then I'm afraid I can't help you. In fact we had no end of trouble after we bought the place because we couldn't find where they'd gone.'

'Oh. Trouble? Why was that?' Hodgkiss inquired.

'Because of all the things they left behind; some of them turned out to be quite valuable. We wanted to send them on but didn't know where. And of course the solicitor wasn't any help ... you know what they're like.'

'What sort of things did they leave behind?'

'Well, there was some quite good furniture. Not really my taste I must say ... it was mostly old-fashioned heavy Victorian stuff that I didn't want around the place. And then there were a few paintings they left in the garage that turned out to be worth quite a lot of money although the frames had been ruined by water.'

'Goodness,' said Hodgkiss chattily, 'one almost gets the impression that the Hardakers must have left in something of a hurry.'

The woman blinked. 'Yes, you could be right. But I'm afraid I can't help you with their present address. Now, if you'll excuse me ...'

When they were in the car Pat turned to Hodgkiss. 'Now what? No. Don't tell me. You want to pay a visit to the relict of the late James Hardaker. Correct?'

Hodgkiss nodded. 'Got it in one. Why not? We have the address and it's only twenty minutes drive from here.'

*   *   *

Sunshine Homes was barely visible from the street.

The main entry, a wide driveway between two towering sandstone pillars surmounted with concrete lions, wound its way through an acre of shrubbery to the rear of the single low long building which had been built in a distant decade to allow for an uninterrupted although distant view of the Pacific Ocean.

Pat found the visitors' parking area at the side of the building and they followed a path between ornamental shrubs to a shallow flight of marble steps leading up to a wide wooden veranda. The front door was a confection or cream-painted wood and coloured leadlights.

An attractive young woman in a blue and white uniform with a cap set at a rakish angle answered Hodgkiss's assault on the electric doorbell.

'We've come to visit Mrs Hardaker,' Hodgkiss announced aggressively.

The young woman, who wore on the breast of her blouse a brooch displaying the name Toovey in italic writing, smiled and nodded.

'Would you like to come in,' she said. 'I'll see if Mrs Hardaker is free for visitors. Just take a seat here.'

She waved a graceful hand towards a well upholstered sofa then disappeared through a green baize door.

Pat took her place on the sofa but Hodgkiss walked quickly across the ringing parquetry floor to a tall window on the far side of the room to take in the impressive panorama of suburban roofs, seafront and ocean.

He had barely begun his inspection when the young woman Toovey returned through the baize door.

'Mrs Hardaker is awake for the present,' she announced. 'Would you like to follow me.'

She held the baize door open for Pat and Hodgkiss to pass through then led the way down a wide corridor with closed doors at intervals on both sides.

She stopped and held open a door on the ocean side of the corridor. She smiled. 'Mrs. Hardaker is not a great conversationalist these days. But you probably know that. Would you like me to bring you some tea or coffee.'

Hodgkiss glanced at Pat who nodded. 'Tea would be nice.'

When Toovey had closed the door silently behind her Pat and Hodgkiss turned to greet the only other occupant of the room; an elderly lady who lay propped up on pillows in a wide, well-made bed with raised iron sides.

The woman appeared to be sleeping, but almost at once her eyes opened. She smiled at them and waved a hand.

Hodgkiss and Pat smiled back and approached the bed cautiously.

But the woman's eyes closed again.

Thus it remained for some minutes.

Soon Pat leaned over and whispered in Hodgkiss's ear. 'Perhaps we should come back later ... this afternoon perhaps. It's not really far to come.'

Then Mrs Hardaker opened her eyes again and said: 'Hello, dears. Glad you could come after all. Pity you couldn't make it last week. We all had such fun.'

'Yes. We're sorry too,' said Hodgkiss, eager to please.

Mrs Hardaker craned her head in an attempt to see behind Hodgkiss.

'Did you bring me something ... a surprise perhaps,' she asked expectantly. 'You know how I love surprises.'

'Unfortunately we were in a bit of a hurry this time,' said Hodgkiss. 'But we'll bring you a surprise when we come next week. All right?'

'Ooooooh! That'll be something to look forward to.'

Mrs Hardaker closed her eyes again and appeared to sleep.

Pat whispered. 'Hodgkiss. Have you seen her ring? And that pendant.'

Hodgkiss nodded. 'Yes. One could scarcely miss them. Are they real, do you think?'

Pat shrugged. 'It's hard to tell. I'd need to take a closer look.'

But at that moment Toovey pushed back the door with an elbow and entered bearing a large silverplate tray with an elaborate porcelain tea pot and delicate cups and saucers. There was also a creamer and sugar bowl with painted flowers.

'How are you getting on?' she asked setting down the tray on a circular glass-topped table with faux bamboo legs.

'Well, she was very chatty when we first came in but she seems to have nodded off now,' Hodgkiss explained.

Toovey nodded. 'Yes. She does that. With you one minute, gone the next.' She picked up the tea pot and began to pour. 'I'll leave you to do the milk and sugar.'

'Excuse me for asking this,' said Pat, 'but I was wondering if it was wise for Mrs Hardaker to be wearing so much expensive jewellery. I mean, very likely she is a little forgetful and might mislay some of it.'

'Or some of the staff might pinch it, you mean,' said Toovey, not at all put out. 'It's not much of a temptation really, you know. It's all fake … costume jewellery.'

'Oh, is it?' said Pat. 'Well, that's a relief, in a way.'

'Yes. The old dear's got tons of it. The settings are quite good, mostly silver. I understand she had them made up herself. She likes to give them away. There was a fellow staying here, used to be a jeweler, he even offered to pay her for a few pieces but she wouldn't hear of it. Mostly they were just stones when she arrived here, they hadn't been set into rings or pendants like she's wearing now.'

'Old family jewels, were they,' Hodgkiss asked.

Toovey chuckled. 'No, nothing of the sort. I've never known whether to believe it or not, but old Lesley, that's Mrs Hardaker, she's always said that her husband found a lot of these jewels, chunks of glass or whatever they are, in an old leather bag when he was digging in the back garden one day.'

'Didn't they ever take them to a jeweler to see if they were real or not? I mean, if jewels like that were real …'

Toovey laughed. 'Oh yes, they did all of that. When her husband first found them he took them to a friend in the antiques trade who said they weren't real gemstones, just paste he called them, whatever that means. So they've always known that they weren't real.'

Hodgkiss asked: 'And the fellow who used to stay here, the jeweler, how many of these paste geegaws did he buy from her, do you know?'

Toovey frowned in concentration. 'I couldn't say for sure, but I know that eventually she got very cross with him because he was always pestering her to sell him more and more of them. Even when he'd left and gone to live interstate, somewhere on the Gold Coast I think it was, he still used to ring up about them. Eventually she told us not to put his calls through. She told us that she wanted to keep the rest of them to give to her grandchildren.'

'Lucky grandchildren,' Pat murmured.

'Well, I'll leave you to have a word with her when she wakes up,' Toovey said, then she left closing the door quietly behind her.

When it became apparent that Mrs Hardaker was not about to wake up again soon Pat and Hodgkiss decided to leave. 'We can call back another time,' Pat whispered. 'It's not far to come.'

They had nearly reached the parking area when they heard footsteps hurrying behind them and they turned to see Toovey approaching, a smile on her face and a small red box in one hand.

'You'd no sooner gone when Lesley woke up and rang for me. She asked where you'd gone and I explained that you'd just left. So she gave me this to give to you,' she said handing the tiny box to Pat.

Pat took the box and opened it. Her mouth fell open. 'But I couldn't possibly accept this,' she said. 'Why it must be three carats. It's beautiful.'

'Well, I suppose you can take it back to her if you like, but I can tell you that it gives her tremendous pleasure handing those things out. And don't worry about it being enormously valuable, they're not real diamonds you know ... none of her things are real.'

Pat sighed and turned to Hodgkiss. 'What should I do?'

'Why don't you take it home and we'll think about it. As you said, it's not far to come back here.'

Pat nodded, dropped the box into her handbag and turned to Toovey. 'Would you please thank Mrs Hardaker very much for me, Toovey, and tell her that we'll call again soon.'

They had been traveling only minutes when the mobile phone in Hodgkiss's shirt pocket buzzed quietly. He took it out and examined the caller's number.

'It's only Donald,' he muttered. 'Do you think I should answer it? It's never good news from Donald, certainly never anything constructive.'

'Of course you should answer it,' Pat snapped. 'It might be important.'

Hodgkiss laughed grimly. 'Important ... Donald. Oh very well then, let's see how important it is.' He opened the connection. 'Yes, Donald. What is it now?'

Donald was speaking hands-free from his unmarked patrol car in the parking area at the rear of the Crestwood police station.

'I thought you'd be interested to know that I've just had a long talk to Roger Ives.'

'Have you indeed. Not a pleasant experience I suspect,' said Hodgkiss with feeling.

'No, but he had quite a bit to say about your friend's problem.'

'My friend's problem?' Hodgkiss queried tartly. 'Which friend and which problem are you talking about, Donald? I have a number of friends with problems.'

'Dad, can you please not be difficult about this. You know very well what I'm talking about. The lady who lived in that house that was flooded.'

'Mina Cumberland, you mean?'

'Yeah. That's the one. Now, why don't you arrange for Pat and her to come home for tea tonight and I might be able to throw some light on the matter for you.'

'That's very thoughtful of you, Donald. I'll arrange it now.' He cut the connection.

'Well, was it important?' asked Pat.

'Could be,' Hodgkiss conceded. 'He said to invite you and Mina for tea and he might be able to throw some light on her problem.'

'Sounds promising,' said Pat.

'Possibly, but knowing Donald it'll probably turn out to be a lot of nonsense.'

Pat turned her head to throw a disapproving look in Hodgkiss's direction but said nothing.

As she pulled the car to a stop outside the Burke's home Pat asked: 'What are we going to tell Donald about ... you know what?'

Hodgkiss turned his head in amazement. 'No, I do not know what. What on earth are you talking about?'

'Well, you don't suppose for one moment that those jewels old Mrs Hardaker has been handing out like lollies were really paste, do you?'

'Really Pat, how would I know? I'm not a gemologist,'

Hodgkiss replied loftily. 'And I don't see how you would know either … not for certain.'

Pat turned off the motor and pulled on the handbrake. 'No, that's true. We don't know for certain, but it's pretty obvious isn't it. Just look at the facts.

'First there is a robbery in which many high quality loose jewels are stolen by the gang that seems to have used Cumberland's place as its headquarters, for some of the time at least.

'Then we know that Cumberland hid them somewhere around the property. Next thing there is a massive flood, or a series of floods, through the Cumberland's place which results in properties at the rear of the Cumberland's also being flooded.

'And let's not forget the "goings-on" in the Cumberland's backyard which Mr Gilbert observed. First, the evening of the planting of the tree during the period of the floods then twenty years later, when we had that big blow which uprooted the tree and led to the removal of Cumberland's remains, or part of them, to the garage.

'Then not long afterwards, when the floods had subsided, a cache of gemstones turns up in the garden of one of the properties downstream from the Cumberlands and it is hardly any time at all before the lucky finders sell up they home with quite remarkable haste and move to a luxury unit with a water view.

'Pretty obvious isn't it, wouldn't you say?'

Hodgkiss shrugged. 'It is certainly possible to construct an hypothesis along those lines. However you must agree that when it is reduced to its elements it is really little more than speculation.'

'"Speculation!"' Pat exploded. 'It's as plain as the nose on your face. What's got into you, Hodgkiss? Now, you listen to me, if you don't tell Donald about this I certainly will. Make no mistake about it. Besides, we have no choice really, unless we want to become accessories after the fact.'

Hodgkiss shook his head. 'Really, Pat, I think you are being a little hasty. Now, ask yourself this; if we expound your theory to Donald what good will come of it? The gemstones are now widely distributed amongst relatives, friends and others, most of whom are under the impression that their gifts are nothing more than pretty but worthless geegaws.'

'Except for one lucky jeweler now living on the Gold Coast who knew damned well what was what.'

Hodgkiss nodded. 'Granted. But tracing all of the gemstones at this stage, twenty years down the track, may prove almost impossible. Besides, no doubt the jeweler who suffered the burglary was insured and the insurance company has paid out on the claim long ago. What purpose would be served by dredging the whole business up again now?'

'"What purpose would be served"?' Pat exclaimed angrily. 'Am I hearing you properly, Hodgkiss? What about the simple principle called *doing the right thing*? You never tire of reminding the boys and girls of Kanundda Council of their duty, or what you think their duty should be. I'm sure Donald would not be in two minds about what to do in this situation.'

Hodgkiss snorted derisively. 'Oh no. Donald would certainly know what to do. He would begin a tedious investigation that with a little luck eventually may lead to the recovery of some of the stones. Then there would be protracted litigation over who actually owned them and who should pay for the costs of the case, and in the end the only winners would be a clutch of greedy lawyers. Is that what you want?'

Pat rolled her eyes and sighed. 'I will leave it to you, Hodgkiss. You decide.'

'Oh thanks. Why is it always left to me to make the tough decisions?' He reached for the door handle.

'Come on in. Esme can make us a sandwich and we can discuss it some more.'

Then he added as an afterthought. 'And when Donald comes home tonight would you mind slipping on the ring Mrs Hardaker gave you.'

'Whatever for?' Pat asked warily.

'Just humour me ... please.'

*　　　*　　　*

Mina arrived punctually at six o'clock, just minutes before Donald turned the unmarked police car in at the driveway.

Pat and Hodgkiss were already settled at the redwood table on the back deck where Esme had set six places for dinner.

Minutes later Donald pulled back the heavy sliding door from the family room and stood to one side to allow Mina to join the others on the deck, then followed, juggling awkwardly a bottle of white wine and four glasses.

He set the glasses down on the table then twisted the top off the bottle and began pouring the wine.

'What about Esme?' Pat asked.

'I asked her if she wanted a drink but she said she'd have one with dinner.' He sniffed cautiously at his wine then sipped.

'Now,' he said; 'Where would you like to start?'

'I think you told Edgar that you might be able to throw some light on Mina's experience,' said Pat. 'Perhaps we should start there.'

'And your interview with Roger Ives,' said Hodgkiss. 'I'd like to hear more about that because I suspect that Ives conduct is at the centre of Mina's problem, isn't that so?'

Donald nodded. 'Yes it is. No doubt about that.'

'Who's Roger Ives?' Mina asked. 'I don't think I've ever heard that name before.'

'No, you wouldn't have,' said Hodgkiss. 'But your unfortunate mother would have been only too familiar the name and with the man himself.'

'So what was his connection with my family?' Mina asked.

'Well, you see, he was working with the Kanundda Council when ...'

Donald cut him off angrily. 'Just hold it there one minute, Dad. Who's telling this story, you or me?'

Hodgkiss raised an eyebrow. 'The trouble with you, Donald, whenever you are put in the position of having to relate a simple set of facts, is that you always ...'

Pat barked. 'Edgar. Be quiet!'

Hodgkiss shrugged, reached for his wineglass and drank.

Donald continued in tightly controlled tones. 'Today I went to the City Central Prison where I spoke to Roger Ives who is serving a life sentence for the murder of an old fellow who used to work for the council.

'That crime has nothing to do with your problem, Mina, because it happened far more recently.

'But he was working for council back in the days when you and your Mum lived in that house.

'His contact with your Mum was over the flooding that happened around that time. Do you remember anything about that?'

Mina shook her head. 'No, I don't remember anything about flooding but now you mention it I do remember that it was raining a lot. And I remember that Mum was always ringing up people and that she seemed to just have one problem after another.'

Donald continued. 'Yes, she certainly had her hands full, poor woman. We know also that your father was keeping very bad company at that time. In fact I know that he was a regular associate of Ives and another fellow by the name of Malcolm Corbett who I've also had several conversations with in the past day or two. Do you remember your Mum ever mentioning the name Corbett?'

Mina frowned in thought then shook her head. 'No. So what did Mum have to do with these people?'

'Ives was the council officer in charge of the new drainage arrangements that caused your property to be flooded.'

Hodgkiss said quietly. 'Donald, that is not correct.'

'Oh, isn't it?' Donald snapped. 'Well, what did he do then?'

'Jan informed me that Ives was given the task of liaising with Mrs Cumberland and others affected by the flooding with a view to ensuring that council's efforts to solve their problem were effective and that they were kept fully informed on what council was planning to do.'

'Well he didn't do much of a job, did he?' said Donald, angry at the interruption.

'Indeed he did not,' said Hodgkiss. 'In fact Ives deliberately did all he could to alarm Mrs Cumberland about the condition of her home. He told her that the torrents of water that had rushed through the foundations had caused such severe damage that the house had become unsafe and may have to be condemned.'

'Well, you got that much right at least,' said Donald. 'In fact Ives admitted to me that he had told Mrs Cumberland that the house would very likely have to be demolished and to underline the fact that it was unsafe he nailed up the doors to most of the rooms at the rear of the house on the grounds, false of course, that it would be dangerous for anyone to even enter them, or so he told her.'

Mina sighed. 'So that's it. That's why I can't remember anything about those rooms … I couldn't get into them because they were nailed up.'

Donald continued. 'Ives told me that there was nothing in any of the nailed-up rooms anyway … no furniture, nothing.'

'A rather odd life-style, wouldn't you say,' Hodgkiss commented. 'Living in a house where only a few of the rooms were furnished. Where did your father sleep, Mina, do you remember that? Not with you and your mother, surely.'

'No. But I suppose there could have been a couch or something somewhere in the house that he used.'

Hodgkiss nodded. 'No doubt. Unfortunately he's not here to tell us. Which reminds me, Donald. Is there anything further on Douglas Cumberland's disappearance?'

'No, not a lot. Ives insists that it was Malcolm Corbett who murdered Cumberland and disposed of the body.'

'Well, he would say that, wouldn't he? What did Corbett say?'

'Nor surprisingly he said he thinks it was Ives that did it, so you can take your pick. I doubt if we'll ever know.'

'And what about the proceeds of the robbery that they were supposed to have quarreled over?'

'Of course I asked Ives about that and he wasn't in two minds about what had happened to the jewels; he was quite sure that Cumberland had hidden them somewhere then pretended that they had disappeared and that was just a trick to rob Corbett and himself of their share.

'He said after the robbery they took the jewels to the

Cumberland's place and Cumberland had hidden them somewhere because they knew that the burglary squad would come looking for them because they'd soon work out that it was Corbett who had done the job and Cumberland and Corbett were well known to be mates.'

'Then one night, after the police had been there, the three of them agreed to divide the jewels up between them then and go their separate ways. Cumberland went out to fetch them and a few minutes later he came back inside in a real state and said that they'd vanished.

'Ives said that it was obvious that Cumberland was putting on an act and that he was just trying to rip off Corbett and himself by making out that somehow the jewels had been stolen.'

Hodgkiss asked: 'And when you spoke to Corbett did you ask him what he though about it … the disappearing jewels?'

'Of course I did. He seemed to think that Cumberland wasn't acting and that somehow the jewels had really disappeared.'

Hodgkiss smiled. 'And what do you think, Donald? Did the jewels really disappear or did Cumberland try to deceive his two accomplices?'

'Of course they didn't disappear. Bags of valuable jewels don't simply disappear overnight. Of course Cumberland tried to rip off the other two and they murdered him for his trouble.'

'And do you intend to charge them … or perhaps one of them and if so which one.'

'At the moment I don't intend to charge anyone over it. We still haven't even got confirmation on the identity of the bones. We've got to establish that first, then when we've done that …'

'Really, Donald, do you doubt for one moment that the bones were those of Mina's father?'

'I'm not in the business of making rash assumptions, Dad. I have to conduct a proper police investigation. One step at a time. But don't worry, I'll get there in the end.'

'I've no doubt you will … eventually. But getting back to the stolen jewels. Where do you think they are now? Have you any idea?'

Donald shrugged. 'No. They could be anywhere. They were only gemstones you know, cut and polished but not made up into pieces of jewellery, so these days you wouldn't even know what to look for. I'd say there's very little chance that they're still just unset stones. It's almost certain that by now someone would have done something with them; made them up into rings or brooches. After twenty years I'd say the chances of finding them would be non-existent.'

Hodgkiss glanced at Pat. 'Yes, I dare say you're right there, Donald. Not much point trying to pursue that aspect of things. Wouldn't you agree, Pat?'

Pat frowned. 'Yes, I suppose so, Hodgkiss, but if Donald decided to make the effort to track them down, well, I'm sure you'd give him any help you could, wouldn't you?'

Before Hodgkiss could reply Donald said: 'I can't imagine that Dad would be much help finding them.'

Hodgkiss nodded. 'On this occasion, Donald, I am unable to disagree.'

Esme, who had stepped out onto the deck in time to hear this last remark, said: 'Well, I'm glad to hear you and Donald agreeing on something, Dad. It doesn't happen often. Now, Donald, if you'd like to come inside I need someone to carve.'

She was about to leave when her eye fell on Pat's hand.

'That's a lovely ring, Pat. Is it new? Where did you get it?'

Before Pat could answer Hodgkiss broke in, laughing. 'Now, that's a good question.' He turned to Donald. 'I'll bet you can't guess where Pat got her new ring.' He continued without waiting for a reply. 'She dug it up in her garden.'

Esme was gobsmacked. 'Oh, Pat you can't have. That's a beautiful stone.'

Donald peered over Esme's shoulder. 'Dug it up, did you Pat. Then I'll bet you it's a brummy. It'd have to be if you found it in your garden.'

'Once again we are in agreement,' said Hodgkiss with emphasis.

* See Hodgkiss and the Fatal Map, *The Hodgkiss Mysteries, Volume 1.*

Hodgkiss and the General Standing Orders

'**Y**es, Hodgkiss. I know I don't *have* to work. I *choose* to work. OK?'

Pat Strong was losing her patience.

'But why? Why work when you don't have to? I don't understand it.' Hodgkiss protested: 'Don't you have enough to occupy your time as it is?'

The two were standing in the kitchen of Pat's comfortable town house in an exclusive cul-de-sac off one of the best streets in Kylerbrin. She was dressed smartly for work and ready to take the short walk to the nearby railway station.

'If by occupying my time you mean waiting around to

dance attendance on your every whim, then the answer is yes, you could most certainly say my time is very fully occupied. However, I want a little more out of life than being your chauffeur and general factotum.'

Hodgkiss feigned indignation. 'Oh, I see. I've become an obstacle to your ambitions; a road-block on your path to fulfillment. Is that it, because that's what it sounds like?'

Pat nodded. 'In a nutshell – yes, it is!'

'Well, I suppose you know what you're letting yourself in for if you go to work at *that* place?' Hodgkiss asked cryptically.

Pat frowned. 'And what's that suppose to mean ... letting myself in for what? It's only the parliamentary library I'm going to work at. I don't think even you, in your wildest excursions into fantasy could find anything suspicious or improper about anything that happens there.'

Hodgkiss raised an eyebrow. 'Do you think not?'

'Come on, Hodgkiss, out with it. What have you heard?'

'It's probably nothing really, but ...' Hodgkiss paused.

Pat exploded. 'Oh, for heaven's sake, Hodgkiss, anything starting with "it's probably nothing really, but ..." is obviously going to be something ... something bad. So what is it? And quickly.'

'Well, seeing that you seem determined to work there I suppose you should know that there are stories doing the rounds about ... well, untoward activities in the parliamentary library.'

'"Untoward activities," Pat quoted. 'Now, that covers a multitude of sins. What sort of "untoward activities?"

Hodgkiss tugged at his short, well-trimmed grey beard. 'It would not be fair of me to point the finger without any definite proof, but ...'

Pat scoffed. 'Really! You've never let that stop you in the

past, so you might as well go ahead and point the finger and be quick about it. I'm already late.'

Hodgkiss drew a deep breath. 'Very well, if you insist. Are you aware that the parliamentary library has recently begun a process of deaccessioning?'

'A process of *what?*'

'Deaccessioning,' Hodgkiss repeated in the tone of one making an explanation of the obvious to a backward child. 'Removing unwanted books from their collection.'

'Really. And how do you know that?'

'One of the staff at the Kanundda Central Library mentioned it to me the other day. She told me that they had been hoping to get their hands on some of the books the parliamentary library is tossing out, but it appears that they have been beaten to the punch.'

'Beaten to the punch by whom?' Pat asked.

'By the trade. Apparently the deaccessioning process has been placed in the hands of one of this city's most rapacious and unscrupulous second-hand book dealers. No doubt he will take all of the best things for himself at a fraction of their value and sell off the rest to his mates in the trade at knockdown rates. I think it's shameful.'

'But if the library's culling their collection surely they wouldn't be getting rid of anything of any real value.'

'Really, Pat, your naivety sometimes disturbs me. What this amounts to is putting Dracula in charge of the blood bank. If the staff at that library had any idea which of their books was valuable and which were not they'd be doing the job themselves, wouldn't they. But the facts are that they haven't got a clue so they've made the mistake of calling in a so-called expert who is going to rob them blind.'

Pat shrugged. 'Well, Hodgkiss, I can only hope that you're

wrong this time because I'd hate to think that the library is going to lose any really valuable books.'

'Then you might be able to help by keeping an eye out while you're at work,' Hodgkiss suggested.

'Keep an eye out for what exactly?'

'Any indications of improper conduct?'

'You mean like people sneaking out with valuable books tucked under their coats.'

Hodgkiss frowned. 'You can make light of it if you like, but you've been warned. You might mention it to some of the others who work there.'

'Oh, wonderful,' said Pat. 'The new girl turns up on day one and tells everyone how to suck eggs. I don't think so, Hodgkiss. Now you've made me so late that I'll have to drive to the station. Do you want me to drop you home first?'

'I suppose so if it's not out of your way.'

'You know jolly well it's out of my way. But come on. I'll be even later if you don't get a move on.'

*   *   *

But in spite of the delay Pat was not late arriving at her new job in the parliamentary library. After dropping off Hodgkiss at the Burke's home in a suburban back street in nearby Lillimoor, Pat found a parking spot near the Lillimoor railway station and was just in time to buy her ticket and join a crowded train as it pulled into the station.

Alighting at Wynyard she climbed the steep rise to Macquarie Street and after showing her new security pass at the entry box made her way to the library at the rear of the parliamentary building overlooking the Domain, with a view across to the Art Gallery.

Upon arriving at the library Pat sought out the head librarian, Raymond Quilty, a short, bearded man with a bald head who had interviewed her for the position.

Quilty introduced her to several of the other workers then showed her to the office where she would work, a small, windowless room with one glass wall and door. A high stack of books on the floor near the desk awaited cataloguing.

Quilty waved an arm at the books. 'I think you know what to do, don't you, Ms Strong.'

Pat nodded. 'I believe so: I'll be checking in the new ones while someone else checks the old ones out.'

Quilty turned to look at her sharply. 'I take it that's a reference to our deaccessioning programme, is it?'

Pat nodded, a little taken aback by the man's sharp tone. 'Yes, a friend mentioned it to me this morning. He heard about it from some of the people at the Kanundda Central Library. Apparently they had hopes of getting their hands on some of the old books you're getting rid of, but found that someone had beaten them to it; professionals in the second-hand trade I think he said. Is that right?'

Quilty nodded stiffly. 'We have an expert in the trade doing the deaccessioning for us; yes, that's true. You can assure your friend that everything is being done openly and transparently.'

He turned stiffly and left the room.

Not the greatest start in my new job, Pat thought, looking about. From where she sat, if she craned her neck to the left, Pat had a view of the library's main office but none of the vista outside.

A woman whom Pat judged to be in her mid-forties, looked up from her desk in an identical glassed-in room across the narrow corridor, smiled, waved, pushed back her chair and rose.

'Carol Wales,' she said entering Pat's office. 'You're the new girl, aren't you. I saw old Quilty in here looking rather grim. Don't worry about him. He's a bit tense at the moment, but he's OK really.'

'I'm glad to hear that,' said Pat. 'I've always thought of libraries as oases of peace and quiet. Why on earth should Mr Quilty be tense?'

Carol lowered her voice. 'It's on account of this deaccessioning business. Old Quilty's been on edge ever since it started.'

'Why is that?' Pat asked innocently. 'Is there a problem with it?'

Carol sat down on the edge of Pat's desk and shook her head. 'There doesn't seem to be anything in particular you could put your finger on, but I know that there's definitely what could be described as "bad vibes" about it. There're suggestions that some of the more high flying book dealers in the trade are getting some pretty good deals on some of the things that are going out for sale.'

'And who is actually in charge of this deaccessioning business?'

'Fellow by the name of Harold Coney.' Carol turned and nodded her head towards the outer office. 'That's him over near the window; the fellow with the long hair.'

Pat leaned across to see into the outer office. A man with long black hair and a bald patch on his pate was seated at a desk beside one of the floor-to-ceiling windows, mobile phone pressed to an ear.

'Well, he certainly has a good view,' she observed. 'So how did he get the job? Does anyone know?'

Carol shrugged. 'That's not for us minnows to know, but we were told that the selection process was perfectly legit and Coney got the job because of his knowledge of books and the book trade. He decides what we don't need any more and should be pitched out. If that's given the OK by old Quilty, then Coney goes ahead and auctions the books off among the leading lights of the second hand book business.'

'Really?' said Pat. 'I must say that sounds like a system tailor-made for rorting. I don't know much about the value of old books but surely some of them must be worth quite a lot and there could well be members of the public who would pay more for many of these books than a second hand dealer who, after all, is just going to on-sell them to the public anyway, and at a handsome profit no doubt.'

Carol nodded. 'You don't have to convince me, but if I was you I wouldn't talk too much about it, not around here anyway. We cataloguers are looked upon as the lowest form of life in the building. No one wants to hear our opinions … especially on the deaccessioning programme.' Carol wriggled off the desk, turned and smiled. 'Let me know if I can help in any way.'

*   *   *

At lunch time Pat took her plastic container of sandwiches to the nearby Botanic Gardens where she settled on a shady seat, opened a pack of fruit juice, took out a sandwich and began eating.

She had just finished her lunch when she saw Coney, the long-haired man who, according to Carol, was in charge of the deaccessioning programme, approaching down one of the many walkways that criss-crossed the area. He was in earnest conversation with a middle-aged woman who Pat remembered was one of the library staff whom Quilty had introduced her to when she arrived that morning.

As Pat watched them approach the woman looked up, saw her and immediately disengaged her hand from that of the long-haired man. As the two passed by the woman glanced at Pat, then looked away and whispered something to her companion who turned back to look over his shoulder.

Pat started to raise a hand in greeting but thought better of it and scratched her nose instead. Then she rose, deposited her drink pack in a rubbish bin and headed back to work.

As she retraced her path towards the rear of the parliament house building she was aware of the other two hurrying close behind her.

By the time she reached the security office at the back entry they were standing close behind her. Pat caused a short delay as she searched in her deep, crowded bag for the security pass issued to all staff and visitors to the building.

The woman behind her said in quiet, friendly tones: 'It helps if you hang it around your neck. Then there's no hold-up at the doors.'

Pat smiled and nodded. She glanced at the photo pass hanging around the woman's neck: Pippa Wright. The man behind her also had his security card attached to a light chain around his neck; Harold Coney.

'I'll do that, thanks, Pippa,' she said, smiling at the woman and her companion. She showed her pass to the uniformed attendant and hurried in.

Pat had slipped easily into the routine of cataloguing the new accessions. The stack beside her desk diminished and when the last one had been entered she rose from her desk and went to the main office. There she found a trolley which she took back to her room, stacked the books and magazines she had catalogued onto its two trays then wheeled it through to the large library area and delivered it to the staff there for distribution to the appropriate shelves.

As she returned to her room she glanced towards where the long-haired Harold Coney sat. He was talking earnestly into a tiny mobile phone. Instead of returning to her office Pat turned and walked towards the tall windows overlooking the domain and within clear earshot of Coney.

Coney did not see her at once and continued his conversation.

'Yes, I know. I realise there are a million and one documents, maps, minutes and assorted items of bum-fodder in this place … but who knows … It could be in there somewhere among all the garbage … it's quite on the cards really. No one's ever seen it that I know of … not for sure. These are just stories. It could be there somewhere so keep your eyes peeled. It's only a little thing … just a few pages. The General Standing Orders it's called … published in 1802. And the fellow I was telling you about, well his name's Wright. Earl Wright. His wife works here with me.'

Then Coney became aware of Pat standing behind him. He swung around to confront her, holding the phone to his shirt.

'Do you mind? I'm trying to have a private conversation here,' he said abruptly.

Pat favoured him with her most winning smile. 'I was just having a little break to enjoy the view. You're so lucky having a window seat.'

Coney scowled. 'Well, I have work to get on with here if you don't mind.'

Pat increased the volume of her smile. 'So sorry, Mr Coney. I wasn't trying to eavesdrop, really. I'll leave you to it then.'

Pat thought she would tell Carol Wales about the man's rudeness but Carol was busy on her phone.

She returned to her room to find that someone had renewed the stack of books beside her desk. She glanced at her watch. 2.45.

She got up and walked around her desk to place her jacket in the metal locker that stood in one corner of the office.

As she returned to her desk she noticed that Carol had finished her call and was typing busily. She glanced out into the main office. Harold Coney, too, was now hard at work, his cryptic conversation ended.

By the time Pat had finished processing the new batch it was time to go home.

*   *   *

Late the next morning Pat was returning to her office from a visit to the toilets when she witnessed an incident that disturbed her.

As she was about to push open the door to her room Pat turned for a last glance at the view through the picture windows before resuming work in the room which she had come to think of as her cupboard.

It was at that moment that she saw Harold Coney about to slip a plastic bag into his briefcase. The bag was not empty. From its clearly defined contours it appeared to contain hard, rectangular items.

Pat acknowledged to herself that this was not a suspicious act in itself. The man was known to be a dealer in books. Indeed this was the purpose of his work in the library.

What she found disturbing was the expression on the man's face as he looked directly at her.

It was a look of mingled anger and guilt.

And what heightened Pat's suspicion was that instead of

putting the plastic bag into his open briefcase, which was obviously his intention, instead Coney immediately placed the bag on a nearby trolley, closed his brief case and put it out of sight under his desk.

Pat entered her room, closed the door and started work, but she was unable to rid herself of the unease caused by what she had witnessed.

As she rose to leave her office at the end of the day she met Carol Wales in the short corridor their offices shared. As they walked together through the building to the front door she told Carol what she had seen.

Carol was rather less concerned than Pat and the subject soon was dropped. Then as Pat felt inside her bag for the security pass she discovered that it was not there.

She laid a hand on Carol's arm. 'Damn. I'm going to have go back. I can't find my pass.'

'You don't need it to go out,' said Carol. 'They're not that strict. I expect they're glad to see the back of us every day. I always think that the security people think of us as just nuisances'

'No doubt,' said Pat. 'But if I don't get it now I'll never be able to get back in tomorrow morning, not without a lot of fuss, and I can do without that.'

Carol nodded. 'That's true. Good night.'

So Pat turned and retraced her steps through the now rapidly emptying building. But when she came to the short corridor leading to her office she was surprised to see Harold Coney standing at her office door. Although the door was open he was not looking into her office but appeared to be looking directly back towards the area where his desk was located at the far side of the main office.

'Are you looking for something, Mr Coney?' Pat inquired politely.

But the man did not reply. He glared at Pat then brushed past her without a word and headed for his desk where he scooped up his brief case and made for the exit.

Pat made a search of her desk but failed to find the pass.

Later, on her way home, she found it in a tiny pocket in the side of her handbag where she usually kept her house keys.

That night she had dinner with the Burkes in the kitchen of their Lillimoor bungalow. She sat beside Hodgkiss on one side of the cramped breakfast nook with Hodgkiss' daughter, Esme and her husband, Detective Inspector Donald Burke, seated opposite.

After they had finished dinner Pat had helped Esme stack the dishwasher, then later, as they sat in the family room with their coffee, she related the incident involving Coney.

'So what's the significance of that, d'you think?' Hodgkiss asked. 'I mean, was there anything particularly suspicious about him being there where you saw him ... at the door to your office?'

Pat nodded her head slowly. 'Yes, I think so. For one thing he had no business to be there. Neither Carol, who works in the only other office on our little corridor, nor I, have anything to do with the programme that he's working on. And ours are the only two offices on that corridor. He had no business there.'

Donald asked: 'All right. So why do you think he was there? Do you have any idea at all?'

'Yes, I think I do. In fact I'm pretty sure I know.' She turned to Hodgkiss. 'You remember what you were telling me the other morning about the deaccession programme?'

'The what?!' Donald demanded.

Pat explained. 'The library's selling off some of the old books and things they don't want any more and Edgar, being a suspicious old sod who sees vice and corruption everywhere, thinks there might be a rort in progress, and I'm very much afraid he might be on the money on this occasion.'

'What do you mean "on this occasion?" I'm usually on the money in matters like this, aren't I?'

'Yes, you have been known to be right,' Pat conceded. 'But why I think you're right this time is because earlier in the day I saw him about to slip a bag of what looked like books into his brief case.'

'But he's there to help the library get rid of old books, isn't he?' Donald objected. 'It's part of his job, isn't it, so there's nothing suspicious about him taking books out of the building, surely?'

Pat frowned. 'Yes, that's perfectly true, Donald. But it wasn't just the fact that he was about to put some books in his bag that worried me; it was the look on his face that really made me wonder. He looked really angry because I'd spotted what he was doing and he also looked guilty as hell, and that could only have been because he didn't want anyone to see what he was up to.'

Donald shook his head. 'That's all pretty thin, Pat. You'd never get a conviction on evidence like that.'

Pat held up a well-manicured hand. 'You wanted to know what I thought was suspicious about him standing at my office door when I came back looking for my pass. Well, the point is that he wasn't looking into my little room at all, he was looking directly out into the main office area … in fact I think he was looking directly at his own desk.'

'And why do you think he was doing that?' Donald asked.

'I think he was testing the line of sight from my office

door to his desk. I think he wanted to check to see if I could actually have seen what he was doing earlier in the day when he was about to put that bag of books into his briefcase.'

'But why would he do that. Surely he would have known if you could have seen what he was doing?'

Pat shook her head. 'Maybe, but not necessarily. You see, there are several desks and filing cabinets and things between my office and where he sits. I think he was checking to see if it had really been possible for me to see exactly what he was up to at the time.'

Hodgkiss nodded. 'That's very interesting, Pat.'

'Oh, and one other thing,' said Pat. 'When I was eating my lunch in the gardens who should come walking towards where I was sitting but Coney and one of the women who works in his area, a woman by the name of Pippa Wright.'

'And what happened.'

'Nothing much. I had the impression that they were rather friendly. They'd been holding hands until she saw me, then she dropped his hand like a hot cake.'

'Are they married, d'you know?'

Pat shrugged. 'They may be, but they certainly aren't married to each other if that's what you mean.'

'And what do you know about these people?'

'About Harold Coney and Pippa? Almost nothing. Remember, I've been there only a couple of days.'

'Then I think it would be a good idea if you did a little digging, wouldn't you agree?'

'Come off it, Dad,' said Donald. 'What's there to dig about? All you've got is the vaguest suspicion ... absolutely nothing, really. OK. So the fellow looked guilty, or so Pat thought. How far away from him were you at the time, Pat?'

Pat frowned in thought. 'Well, I'm not much good at

distances, Donald, but I assure you I was close enough to see exactly what he was doing and the expression on this face, and it was not pleasant. He certainly didn't like me seeing what he was up to.'

'OK,' Donald conceded, 'but it doesn't mean that he was up to anything illegal, does it? He might have looked cranky for some totally different reason.'

Hodgkiss interrupted. 'Really, Donald, I don't know why you're defending the fellow when he's obviously been up to no good.'

'There you go again; everything's always so obvious to you, isn't it? Well, I don't see anything obvious about it … not obviously crooked anyway.'

'No, Donald, I wouldn't expect you to and that's because you are not in possession of the facts.'

Donald rolled his eyes. 'And you are, I suppose.'

'I am in possession of certain facts that lead me to believe that all is not as it should be at that place.'

'Ah! It's only *certain* facts now, is it? And what might these certain facts be, if it's not too much to ask, although I've no doubt it's to do with this deaccessioning business, right'?

'Of course it is. The entire programme is tailor-made for corruption and Pat's observations only re-enforce that view.'

'Her observations about seeing this fellow putting something in his bag, d'you mean?'

'Yes. That among other things.'

'Other things. What other things. What on earth are you talking about now?'

'The fact that I had been forewarned by contacts at our local library that all was not well with this deaccessioning process.'

'Oh. And how would they know that. What has it got to

do with our local library.'

'They were interested in acquiring some of the books that were to be sold off but when they made inquiries they soon discovered that they were frozen out because all the best books were being flogged off to the chums of the fellow in charge of the process, this Harold Coney.'

'But there wouldn't be much in it for them anyway, would there?' said Donald. 'I mean, the books they're getting rid of, they're only old books that nobody wanted, isn't that true, otherwise they wouldn't be throwing them out, right? And even I know that just because a book's old doesn't mean that it's valuable, or that's what I've heard you say often enough when you've come back from the garage sales with a bundle of books.'

Hodgkiss nodded. 'True, Donald. With books age doesn't necessarily equate to value. In fact the reverse is quite often the case. Nevertheless it is highly likely that there are books of considerable value in the old archives of the parliamentary library. Their stocks go back to the very earliest days of our colony. There could be extremely valuable old books and other documents there and no one would know about them until this Coney fellow happened to unearth them.'

'Is that true, Pat?' Donald demanded.

'Yes, I suppose there could be some pretty valuable old things there. Not only books mind you, but also old maps, pamphlets … things like that. I guess you'd need to be a bit of an expert to recognise the value of some of the things when you came across them.'

Hodgkiss nodded grimly. 'Yes, and no one will ever know what's there except for this Coney fellow because he's in sole charge of the whole operation. Isn't that so, Pat?'

'Well he certainly appears to be. Oh, and there's another

thing I've just remembered; while I was standing near Coney's desk enjoying the view from the big picture windows I couldn't help overhearing something he said. I don't know who he was speaking to and I can't remember his exact words but it was something like, *there are millions of the things there and who knows what might be among them.* But I do remember he said one thing that made me think that he was interested in finding something in particular. He said: *Even so the bloody thing might not be here. No one's ever seen it that I know of. These are just stories.* I'm sure he used those exact words. I made a point of remembering them because it sounded to me as if he had something definite in mind.'

'Well, that clinches it,' said Hodgkiss. 'They're on the lookout for something in particular and we can be sure that it's something rare and valuable.'

'Oh, c'mon, Dad,' said Donald. 'I still reckon you're both making something out of nothing.'

'Do you indeed, Donald,' said Hodgkiss peevishly. 'First, we have the man's obvious guilt at being detected in the act of attempting to conceal stolen articles in his briefcase; secondly we have him checking the line of sight from Pat's office door to his desk to test whether or not she could have seen exactly what he was up to and thirdly we have the text of part of his telephone conversation with an unknown accomplice which makes it quite clear what they're about, and you say it's nothing. Well, Donald, I'd say we have plenty of grist for our mill; plenty of data on which to begin an inquiry.'

'But I don't see how we can do anything about it,' said Pat. 'I just work there, Hodgkiss. I can't go around asking people who aren't connected with my job a whole lot of questions that have no bearing on what I'm supposed to be doing there.'

'Maybe not,' Hodgkiss conceded. 'But you can keep an eye

on that Coney fellow at least. You stopped him once from running of with what was very probably a bagful of valuable books or documents. Just keep an eye on the fellow.'

*   *   *

That bloody woman. Why on earth did she have to look across at me just as I was about to put those damn things in my bag.

But in fact Harold Coney was more angry with himself than he was with that new woman who worked in cataloguing; what was her name … Pat someone … Pat Strong. Yes, that was it. Not bad looking either.

Just the same it was a bit of a worry. He'd have to be more careful in future.

Harold was standing on the footpath at the rear of the parliament house building, uncertain what to do.

He did not want to over-react to what could be a totally insignificant occurrence. But nor did he want to dismiss it if it had the potential for creating problems.

Harold decided the potential was there. He reached into his shirt pocket, took out his mobile phone and called up a number

'Pippa? Where are you?'

'I'm still at my desk. I was just about to leave.'

'Can you meet me out the back for a moment? I won't keep you.'

'What is it? Is something wrong?'

'No. Why do you ask?'

'It's just that you sound anxious.'

'I'm fine. It's not a problem … really. Can you come?'

'I'll be there in two minutes.'

'What is it? 'Pippa asked when she arrived slightly out of breath. 'Nothing serious, I trust.'

Harold shook his head. 'It's that new woman in cataloguing. The one we saw in the gardens at lunchtime.'

'Yes, I remember. What about her?'

'It's nothing really, but she just happened to look straight in my direction just as I was about to slip a couple of nice maps and things into my bag.'

'That's a problem?' Pippa asked, incredulous. 'It could have been your lunch or something; a magasine, anything. A present you were taking home to your Mum.'

'Yes, I realise that,' he said crossly. 'But there was something about the way she looked at me. Then I caught her hanging around behind me while I was on the phone to Carol.'

'You think she was listening in?'

'No, not really. Possibly. I'm confused about it. Anyway I got rid of her. She wouldn't have overheard anything that meant much to her.'

'What were you talking to Carol about?'

'Oh, just what Earl had told me to say. That she should keep an eye out on the things that come through for cataloguing. I told her what it looked like; that we didn't even know if it was there even. Or if it really existed. She asked how valuable it was and I told her it was worth a lot of money. That's all. I told her about Earl and how keen he was to get his hands on it.'

'Was that wise?'

'I don't see why not. If she finds it we're going to have to deal with her about it. She's not altogether silly, you know. She and that Pat Strong woman, they have to read at least the titles of all the things they process. She'd be sure to recognise that it was somewhat out of the ordinary and if she took it to Quilty to ask him how to catalogue it we'd never get our hands on it then, would we?'

'I suppose not. So that's all you wanted to say, is it?'

Harold shook his head miserably.

'No. There's another thing. After Pat Strong left for the day I went over to her room to check if she could really have seen what I was doing when she looked in my direction and, just my luck, she came back and saw me there.

'Saw you doing what? Just standing there?'

Harold nodded. 'Yes. Standing there.'

'So what did she say … anything?'

'She just asked what I was doing.'

'And what did you say?'

'I didn't say anything. I just bolted, grabbed my bag and came out here.'

Pippa paused. 'So what do you want me to do about it?'

'You'd better tell Earl, I suppose. He'd better know just in case anything comes of it.'

'I can't see how anything can come of it, but I'll tell him if you like.'

'Fine. Have you got time for a drink?'

Pippa glanced at her watch, turned and smiled. 'Time for a quick one. Drink I mean.'

*   *   *

Pippa's husband, Earl Wright, treated her news with caution.

'So Coney's worried this woman might have seen something?'

'Worrying about nothing, said Pippa. 'He's the nervous type.'

'What do you know about this Pat Strong woman?' Earl asked as they stood in the kitchen of their flat, sipping sherry before dinner.

Pippa turned and rested her hip against the island bench. 'I know nothing about her. She's been at the library for two days. She's one of the two women on cataloguing. Ray Quilty decided it was time to catch up on ten years backlog of uncatalogued periodicals, new accessions and assorted junk mail.'

'So who hired her?'

Pippa shrugged. 'Quilty did, I suppose. He does most of the hiring.'

'Then can you find out something about her from this Quilty fellow ... where he got her from? Was the job advertised ... things like that?'

'Do you really think it's a good idea? If we start asking questions about her ...'

Earl nodded. 'I see what you mean. Does anyone else there know her?'

'Not that I'm aware of. I saw her talking to Carol Wales. She's the other cataloguer. Their offices are opposite each other off the same little corridor.'

'Well, can you ask her?'

Pippa shrugged. 'I suppose so, but I can't think why Carol'd know anything about her.'

'You never know; she might have recommended her or something.'

'OK. I'll ask around.'

'Discreetly!'

'Yes.'

He asked abruptly. 'Had you been drinking before you came home tonight?'

'It's none of your business, Earl, but yes, I had a drink with one of the girls from the front desk.'

Earl grimaced sourly. 'I thought I smelled drink on your breath when you came in.'

He paused, sipped his sherry, then continued. 'I'm beginning to think it was a mistake putting Harold Coney in there to do this job for us.'

'You didn't have a lot of choice, did you,' said Pippa. 'Your friend Ferdie had a criminal record so Quilty wouldn't have had him at any price.'

Earl nodded gloomily. 'The way Harold behaved today showed a distinct lack of astuteness. He should be more cautious when he's talking on the phone.'

'Well he wouldn't have been talking to that Wales woman at all if you hadn't told him to warn her to be on the look out for it. You ring him too often anyway. We're not supposed to have private calls at work.'

'I have to keep track of what he's doing. If I didn't ring from time to time he'd never get the job done.'

'I don't agree. He's really getting through the stacks down stairs and if there's anything to be found that's where it'll be.'

'And his silly exercise trying to test what that woman might have been able to see when he was going to put things in his bag ... and getting caught doing it...' Earl snorted unpleasant. 'The man's a fool.'

Pippa sipped her sherry. She was not about to argue with him. 'He's right you know; that thing you've got everyone on the lookout out for ... it's probably not there. No one's ever seen it as far as I know. I'm sure most of them have never even heard of it.'

'It's there,' Earl said in what was nearly a shout. 'It must be there. I know someone who's seen it. And he knew what he was looking at.'

'If he saw it then he'd be able to tell you where it is, wouldn't he?'

Earl shook his head. 'He saw it before they had the flood

with the sprinklers. After that everything was moved around. That's why no one at that place knows where to find anything anymore.' He shook his head in disgust. 'Lot of damned incompetents.'

Pippa said softly. 'They're not as incompetent as you think, most of them.'

Earl smiled unpleasantly. 'Found a friend, have you. Was your drinking partner this evening from the front desk ... a man perhaps?'

Pippa turned away. 'Don't start that again, Earl.'

But Earl strode across the kitchen to confront her. 'Don't think you can deceive me, Pippa,' he said, menace in his voice. 'And don't forget, no drinks with friends tomorrow. I want you home early. We'll have work to do ... some signing.'

Pippa opened her mouth to protest, then thought better of it.

*   *   *

The following day, at lunch time, Pat was once again sitting in the gardens, her plastic lunch box beside her resting on the slats of the bench seat, a small container of fruit juice, bent straw in place in one hand, when she looked up to see Pippa Wright standing beside her.

Pat raised a hand. 'Hey, there.'

Pippa sat beside her. 'Do you want some company?' she asked, 'although it's a bit late if you don't, eh?' she added with a smile.

'I'd love some company,' said Pat not altogether truthfully. She added: 'I sense this is company with a purpose.'

'Well, you're not easy to fool. Yes, there is something I need to talk to you about.'

'Can I guess what it's about?' Without waiting for an answer Pat continued. 'Harold Coney and the deaccessioning. Am I right?'

Pippa looked at her sharply then nodded. 'Yes. What made you think that, although I'm hardly surprised.'

'Harold seemed a bit on edge yesterday. There was definitely something odd in the air, although I've no idea what it was exactly.' She paused before continuing guardedly. 'I've a feeling this may be one of those cases where 'tis folly to be wise.'

'You may be right at that. Do you mind telling me how you came to get your job here?'

'Not at all. About five years ago I did some cataloguing work in one of the university libraries. Mr Quilty contacted my old boss looking for someone with experience and he recommended me for the job.'

'Simple as that, eh?'

'Simple as that. Anything else you'd like to know?'

Pippa shook her head.

'Then perhaps there's something you can tell me. Do you know how Harold Coney got the job of doing the deaccessioning?'

Pippa replied casually. 'I understand that he's very well-known in the second-hand book trade. He's supposed to be particular expert on early Australian books, documents, maps ... things generally.'

'Is he? But surely there are others, probably quite a few others, who could have done the job just as well. When he was appointed wasn't there just a little concern about someone from the trade being put in charge. To quote a friend of mine, it's like putting Dracula in charge of the blood bank.'

Pippa smiled. 'I've heard that said before about Harold. I

know there're quite a few people whose noses were put out of joint when he was given the job.'

Pat sipped her drink. 'I can believe that. From what I've heard there're more than a few local council libraries who would have loved to get their hands on some of our rejects before they went out to the trade.'

'I dare say you're right. Well, you know what they say about eggs and omelettes.'

'I do indeed. Nevertheless I think it's unfortunate that things have been arranged in this way. I understand that you're helping Harold in getting the job done. Do you have a background in the second-hand book trade too?'

'Not me, but my husband, Earl, is what I believe is called a bibliophile.'

'Is he now. Then I'd say that Mr Coney and your good self are very well placed to assist your husband in his hobby, or perhaps I should say obsession. My experience has been that people who are avid collectors of anything usually become more than a little obsessional.'

'Are you a collector too, Pat?'

Pat shook her head. 'No, not me, but I have a friend who collects watches … with great enthusiasm. Unfortunately his pockets aren't deep enough to enable him to purchase items from the very top shelf. And what about your husband: do his means enable him to reach for the top shelf?'

Pippa nodded. 'Yes, but it's complicated. My husband Earl has no money of his own, yet he has access to tons of it.'

Pat raised an eyebrow. 'Really! Lucky man. Sounds intriguing.'

'Intriguing is not what I'd call it. Damned inconvenient is more like it because it involves me in doing a lot of things I'd rather have nothing to do with.'

'That's rather cryptic,' said Pat. 'Would you care to explain? You needn't if you don't want to.'

'It's no big secret. Half the people at work know about our situation. You can't keep anything quiet around here. Earl is an undischarged bankrupt. He's not supposed to have any money of his own and of course he doesn't … legally. But he still gets easy access to as much as he wants which involves me in a lot of work.'

'Signing documents, you mean?'

'Exactly. And not only documents.'

'Cheques too, no doubt.'

Pippa nodded. 'It's been this way for years because he's designed his whole life around being a bankrupt and of course that makes me the lifeline between him and his money, or rather my money. That's the way he arranged things with the money from the poor people who he ripped-off. I'm often, too often, presented with a stack of documents to sign and I've no idea what they mean, most of them. Once, when I asked if I could have a particularly long and complicated form explained to me so I'd know exactly what it was I was signing, he nearly went through the roof. So these days I just do as I'm told and sign the jolly things. It's just not worth the trauma fighting him over it although I'm frightened that one day the police will come and take me away for signing something I shouldn't have. Unfortunately the whole awful mess has soured things between the two of us. He knows he has to rely on me to do this and he's become resentful about it although that's the way he's arranged it, and of course I've become resentful about having to do it. And all completely in the dark. Not good for a relationship.'

'So I've noticed.'

'Harold and me you mean … holding hands.'

'Well, you weren't being exactly secretive about it. Does your husband know?'

'He doesn't know about Harold, but he suspects that there might be someone.'

'Is it possible that your husband was instrumental in having Harold given this job? Again you needn't answer, but it occurred to me that he, as a collector, and Harold, as a dealer, may well have had contacts in the past.'

'There's not much gets past you, is there, Pat. Yes, Earl arranged the job for Harold.'

Pat took a bite of her sandwich then asked cautiously: 'Do you know that I accidentally overheard a conversation Harold was having on the phone the other day while I was admiring the view?'

Pippa nodded. 'Yes, I heard all about that. Do you mind telling me what you overheard?'

'I didn't deliberately eavesdrop but I couldn't help hearing what he was saying although it didn't make a great deal of sense.'

'Did he mention anything in particular; a book or some document?'

Pat shook her head. 'No, I'm quite sure of that. I'd have remembered it if he had. But from what he said it seemed that he was looking for some book in particular but wasn't really sure if it was there. Would that be right?'

'Yes, it's very likely he said something along those lines because they *are* searching for a particularly document; a very rare little publication. In fact it's the very first item printed in Australia.'

Pat's eyebrows shot up. 'Goodness. That'd be worth having for a collector.'

'It'd be worth having for anyone,' said Pippa. 'You could

name your own figure. Book collectors around the world would fight for it. You'd be looking at hundreds of thousands of dollars.'

'And what's the name of this priceless book?'

'Well, it's not really a book and it hasn't even got a proper name. It was printed in 1802 and it was just a collection of all the standing orders issued by the various governors up to that time. I think it's just called the New South Wales General Standing Orders.'

'It doesn't sound very exciting.'

'No, it doesn't, does it? But what would be exciting would be owning it. Earl says the records say that there're only three copies in the world. Two in the Mitchell Library and one in a library in England somewhere.'

'But he believes that there's a fourth copy, does he, and that it's here in our library?'

'Believes is the operative word. Of course he doesn't *know* although he says he knows someone who claims to have seen it.'

'What about Harold? Does he believe it's there too? He didn't sound convinced from what I overheard of his conversation with your husband; assuming it was your husband he was talking to.'

'No. Harold is by no means convinced that it's there but he doesn't mind looking for it because he has to search through all that old stuff anyway to find anything worth flogging off to the trade.'

'And has he managed to find much that's been worth selling?'

'Oh yes, quite a lot. Of course most of it is just old records of things that have little or no interest to anyone, but amongst it all he's found some quite valuable things; particularly books and magazines with interesting illustrations. That's what the book trade will pay good money for.'

'And he gives the money back to the library I assume.'

'Oh yes, after he takes a healthy commission.'

Pippa glanced at her watch. 'I'm sorry I've taken up all of your lunch time with my chatter. We'd better get going it we don't want to be late. I'll give you a start. I don't think we should be seen arriving back together looking all chummy.'

*   *   *

'I'm sorry that we've got to do it like this … here in my old car.'

'Don't worry about that, Harold. I rather enjoy it. It takes me back to my teen years.'

In the back of the small dark car Coney looked in surprise at Pippa Wright, who was snuggled semi-naked against him. 'You used to do it often in cars, did you? When you were younger?'

'Oh, yes.' she said casually. 'I hope you're not too shocked. In those days my boy friends usually didn't have the money to take me to a motel or somewhere like that.' Pippa wriggled, manoeuvering awkwardly to reach her underwear which had fallen onto the floor of the cramped rear compartment. She rubbed a bare forearm against the window that had fogged over with their breathing, and looked out into the dark. She added as an afterthought: 'Or perhaps they just didn't think enough of me to want to spend the money.'

In the dark car Harold Coney flushed crimson. 'Well, I suppose I could book us into a hotel somewhere, but we'd have to check in and out, and that'd waste time, then there'd be all the business of booking in and and …'

Pippa laughed and took his hand. 'I didn't mean for you

to take it personally like that. I told you, I like doing it with you in the car. I think it's more exciting than skulking off to some seedy hotel somewhere. And it saves time.' She glanced at her tiny watch. 'We'll have to get a move on. Earl will put me through the third degree again if I'm too late home.'

They were silent as both replaced their discarded clothes then climbed out of the car and took their places in the front seats.

Then unexpectedly Harold announced bluntly. ''I found his ruddy book this afternoon … if you can call it a book. It's really nothing more than a pamphlet.'

Pippa turned to look at him in amazement. 'The General Standing Orders! You've actually found them!?'

He nodded, looking ahead grimly through the windscreen at the dark bushland.

'Why on earth didn't you tell me before?'

'I didn't want to spoil our evening together.'

'Spoil our evening! How would telling me that have spoiled the evening?'

'It means that Earl will get what he wants … he seems to always get what he wants.'

'Well, there's no reason why he should this time.'

'Oh he'll get it alright. He wanted to come around to my place tonight to pick it up straight away, but I told him I didn't have it …that I hadn't taken it from the library yet.'

'D'you mean you've already told him that you've found it?'

Harold nodded.

'Oh, Harold, why did you do that?'

Surprised, he turned to look at her. 'Why did I tell him? Well, he had to know didn't he?'

'Why?'

'But that was the whole point of him getting me the job; to look for the standing orders.'

'So what. That doesn't mean you've got to meekly hand the thing over to him.'

'I don't intend to do that. He's going to have to pay.'

'How much? Have you put a figure on it yet?'

'No. Not yet. I've got to think about that.'

'Harold, there's a number of things you've got to think about, starting with why should you hand it over to Earl at all. There're a thousand book collectors out there who'd fight each other to the death to get their hands on that thing. You know that. Why should you give Earl the inside running?'

'But ...'

'And please don't tell me that you owe it to him because he got you the job. He wasn't doing you a favour. He was using you ... using you as his ferret to dig the thing out for him. Don't you see that? You owe him absolutely nothing.'

Harold nodded abstractedly. 'Yes. I suppose you're right. But a deal's a deal, isn't it. Besides I can make him pay through the nose for it. I don't think he'd argue. He's really crazy to get his hands on it.'

'So where is it now?'

'I put it back in the same stack where I found it. It's buried between some old copies of a boring old periodical that nobody has looked at for donkey's years. Don't worry, I've got the spot well marked. I'll have no trouble finding it again. And I've made a couple of photocopies of it. I'll show one to Earl when I see him tomorrow. I thought it wouldn't be wise to have the original with me while we discussed price, but I know he'll have to be convinced that I've actually found it before he'll even talk money.'

'But you'll have to get it out of the building eventually, and the sooner the better, and without that Pat Strong woman seeing you popping it into your briefcase.'

Harold smiled grimly. 'That won't happen again. I promise you that. Here's the copy. Would you like to see it?'

Pippa nodded and Harold reached across and opened the glove compartment. 'Is that it?' she asked, obviously disappointed with the few sheets of stapled photocopies that he handed to her. 'I'd say it's a helluva disappointment. And from the look of this I'd say that the condition doesn't look great either.'

'No. It's not very impressive, but that's hardly surprising really. After all, you could hardly expect them to have run off Gone With The Wind. They had just one primitive little wooden printing press that came out with the first fleet and they were lucky to have a convict by the name of Howe who, as luck would have it, just happened to be a printer by trade. I suspect that even this modest effort must have taken Mr Howe quite some time to set up and run off the few copies they made at the time.'

'Well I'm sure Earl will find it very impressive. When do you plan to show this to him?'

'Tomorrow night probably, if he can wait that long. I told him I'd ring him in the morning.'

'Personally I think you're crazy. Why give him first go at it when you could almost certainly get lots more from some other collector? There are people in the States who would pay you much more than Earl could raise.'

'Yes, and I could probably get much more if I gave it Sotheby's to auction off, but they're sure to want to know where I got it from. That's the catch of course. And if I tried to pull a swift one on Earl he'd blow the whistle on me rather than let me sell it to someone else. If that happened I could easily finish up in gaol.'

'You might have a point,' Pippa conceded unwillingly. 'Well, I suppose we'd better make tracks.'

She leaned across to deliver a long, hard kiss.

*   *   *

Earl was in earnest conversation on his mobile phone when Pippa arrived home, so she was able to slip unnoticed into the bathroom to check her clothes and make up.

On her way to the kitchen she paused at the door to Earl's study. He was standing facing the window with his back to the door, tiny phone pressed to an ear. She stood in the hall-way, listening.

'Tomorrow. He said he'd be ringing me about it tomorrow. He's found it all right, or he says he has. Personally I'll believe it when I see it. It's hard to believe that a simpleton like Harold Coney could have succeeded where others have had no luck.' (A short pause.) 'No, he didn't say exactly where he'd located it, but with the job I arranged for him he's got a pretty free hand to look where he pleases throughout the whole damned place.' (Another pause.) 'No, he hasn't brought it out yet. That'll be tomorrow. He said he'd ring mid-morning and if I haven't heard from him by eleven I'll ring him. I'm not going to let this slip away.' (Pause.) 'No, we haven't discussed price yet. Of course I've got a figure in mind and knowing Coney as I do he'll think he's going to be able to hold me to ransom. If he tries that he's going to get an unpleasant surprise. I won't take any nonsense from him over this. (A long pause.) Of course, it's not easy to put a price on something like this. It's unique. There's never been a sale for one of them so it's anybody's guess within certain parameters, but it's got to be around a million. I know that there are those who'd pay more but of course the difficulty is the provenance. You understand that of course. It could never be put up for sale in the normal course. Who's going to be able to come up with a credible story of how they came by it? You could try to say it was in great-grandfather's chest in the attic but who's going to buy that? No, it's a big problem from that point of view, but don't you worry, between the two of us we're going to get there. (Pause.) Oh don't worry about Coney, I can take care of him. And if he starts to play funny buggers I know how to handle that too. Yeah! Be in touch.'

Earl disconnected and turned to see his wife standing in the doorway to the hall.

'Oh, you've decided to come home have you? What happened? Your boyfriend kicked you out, did he?'

Pippa turned and hurried on to the kitchen, Earl hard on her heels.

'I suppose he's told you, has he?' Earl demanded.

'Who's told me what?' Pippa replied aggressively. 'I don't know what you're talking about.'

'Don't play games with me. You must think I'm stupid. I simply asked if your friend Coney told you that he's finally found my book.'

'Of course not. He doesn't tell me a thing.'

'Then it'd be news to you, would it; that he's found the General Standing Orders ... or he says he's found it.'

'Yes, it's news to me. When did he tell you?'

'This afternoon.'

'So when are you going to see him to get it?'

'He's going to ring me in the morning when he's got it out of the library.'

'Then you shouldn't count your chickens. He could get

caught trying to take the thing out. There's a new woman working there who's keeping a sharp eye on him.'

Earl nodded. 'Yes. I heard about her. Do you know her?'

Pippa shook her head. 'I know her by sight and I know where she works. She's in a good position to keep an eye on everything Harold does. He can't breathe without her noticing.'

'You don't really think she'll be a problem, surely. She can't watch him every minute of the day. He's only got to keep his eye on her and be careful how he goes about it. The book itself is only a tiny thing. I don't see how it could possibly be a problem.'

'It should be OK then, shouldn't it?' said Pippa. She continued. 'I couldn't help hearing what you were saying to Artur just now, I assume it was Artur you had on the phone; and it sounded to me like you were planning to on-sell it to him. Is that right? After all the trouble you've gone to get your hand on the thing are you really planning to sell it?'

'That's my affair. If I do decide to sell it it's none of your business, except of course you'll just have to do your usual thing. Sign the papers when I ask you to and keep your mouth shut about it. Right?'

She turned away. 'I always have in the past.'

He moved hurriedly to confront her. 'What's that supposed to mean ... you always have *in the past*? Is that some kind of a dumb threat?'

'Does it sound like a threat, does it? Then perhaps it is. You really believe you can go through life bullying everyone into doing whatever you want, don't you? Look at the way you've bullied me into signing all those papers just so you can cheat your creditors out of their money.'

'I don't cheat anyone out of anything.'

'Oh I know it's all legal ... but it stinks. And just because you bully me into doing what you want it doesn't mean that everyone's going to let you have your way.'

Earl smiled unpleasantly. 'Ah ha. I think I'm beginning to understand. Are you telling me that your little pansy friend Harold is going to try to pull a fast one on me? If that's what he's got in mind then perhaps you'd like to give him a message for me.'

Without another word he drew back his hand and struck her a stinging blow across the cheek.

'That's what your little friend Harold will get if he tries any nonsense with me, except it won't be with an open hand. And that won't be all. Will you tell him that when you see him.'

Pippa held a hand to her cheek, her eyes glaring with hate.

'You're a bully, Earl, and a thief. I only hope I live to see the day when you get what you deserve.'

She turned and hurried from the room.

Minutes later Earl heard the front door slam then the sound of Pippa's car start up in the driveway.

*　　*　　*

Pippa and Harold had showered together then rubbed each other dry.

Now they were dressing in Harold's shabby bedroom, cramped by the towering pieces of Victorian mahogany furniture he had inherited from his parents.

Later they made coffee and drank it on the tiny north-facing balcony off the kitchen.

'So when are you going to ring him ... ring Earl?' Pippa asked as they carried their mugs back to the kitchen.

'Mid-morning I said. I'll do it around ten.'

Pippa ran cold water into her mug. 'I still think you're crazy for just handing it to him. Think about it, Harold. You could do so much better.'

Harold sighed. He was tired of discussing this. 'Look, Pippa, you're probably right, I could get more for it from someone else. But if I do that Earl would go straight to the police and tell them that I stole it. Then where'd I be?'

'But you could deny it. And there'd be no way he or the police or anyone could prove it was stolen. Earl need never know who you sold it to. No one at the library knows any-thing about it. Certainly the person you sold it to wouldn't want to make trouble.'

Harold shook his head. 'It's just all too difficult. Keep it simple; sell it to him, take his money and leave it at that. No complications.'

Pippa grimaced. 'I just hate to see the bastard get every-thing he wants.'

'Then maybe I should ring him and tell him the deal's off.'

'I wish you would, but he'll still want to have it now that you've told him you've actually found the thing.'

'Then I'll ring him now, arrange for him to come here now and get it over and done with.'

'But you can't do the deal now anyway; you haven't got the book here.'

'No, and I'm not about to bring it out until I've done a deal with Earl or someone else and we've settled on a price.'

'Well, you'd better make sure that he understands that he's only coming to see some photocopies otherwise I warn you, he'll do his block. He thinks when you ring this morning you'll already have the book here.'

'All right then. I'll just make sure he knows what he's going to see ... a photocopy.'

Harold went to the bedroom to make the call. Minutes later he was back.

'Well?' Pippa asked.

'I told him that he would be seeing only a photocopy and then, if he's satisfied it's what he thinks it is then I'll bring the real thing out and we could do the deal. He wasn't pleased.'

'I'm not surprised. Did you discuss price?'

Harold shook his head. 'Not yet. He wants to see the photocopy before he mentions a figure. He says he needs to know what condition it's in; how many pages, what's actually in the standing orders; is it an interesting read.'

'So when is he coming?'

'He's on his way now.'

'What! Then he'd better not find me here when he arrives. I'll wait in the coffee shop over the road. I'll be able to see from there when he leaves.'

She kissed him firmly on the mouth and headed for the front door. Harold watched her hurrying across the road, pausing to turn and wave in the direction of the flats. He saw her take a seat at a table in the picture window at the front of the coffee shop and wave again. She put on a pair of dark glasses.

Harold had to wait only ten minutes before Earl Wright's distinctive sports car turned in off the street and disappeared down the ramp into the basement car park. In little more than a minute the brass knocker on the front door of his flat was assaulted with a prolonged tattoo of violent blows.

Harold glanced through the spy hole then opened the door.

'I don't intend to waste time with you over this, Harold,' Earl said without preamble. 'Have you got it here?'

'Earl, I just told you on the phone not ten minutes ago; I haven't brought it out yet.'

'Why the hell not?' Earl barked, following Harold into a lounge at the front of the building. 'I'm wasting my time dealing with you. I should have got someone else to do the job.'

'Yes, perhaps you should,' Harold agreed mildly. 'Do you want to see it or not … this photocopy I made.'

'Well I suppose I'd better see it … I'm here now. I don't want the visit to be a complete waste of time.'

Harold turned to a side table under the front window that looked over the street. He opened a drawer and took out a brown envelope. He handed it to Earl. 'That's it … a copy of it,' he said, then added: 'Not very impressive in itself.'

Without a word Earl pulled the flap open then drew out the stapled photocopied sheets. He examined these carefully, taking time to read each page.

'Well, you're right about that. Not very impressive at all. From the look of these I'd say the condition is poor and the content is extremely dull.' He paused. 'Now, down to business. When do you think you can … er, liberate the real thing from the library.'

'Any time. There'll be no problem about that. As you see, it's only small. Fit in my jacket pocket.'

'You wouldn't want to fold it.'

'Of course I'm not going to fold it. What do you take me for?'

'I'll take that as a rhetorical question, Harold, because I'm quite sure that you already know exactly what I take you for. You wouldn't be flattered.'

Harold flushed. 'If you take me for a thief then it's you that's made me one.'

Earl decided not to pursue the subject. 'OK. Let's suppose you can get the thing out tomorrow without being caught; how much do you want for it?'

'That's not easy to say, Earl. There're no previous sales to give me a guide.'

'I know that,' Earl snapped. 'Give me a ball-park figure.'

'A million.'

Earl's jaw dropped. 'In the words of a certain well-known film character: "you're dreaming."'

'Dreaming or not, that's my price. I'm the one taking the risks. If I'm caught smuggling it out of the building it's not you that'll go to gaol.'

'But you told me just now how easy it'd be. It's only little, you said. No problem. So unless you're a complete imbecile you won't get caught.'

'No, I dare say I won't. But tell me this; why should I give you the inside-running on it. There're plenty of other collectors who'd give their back teeth for it … as you well know.'

Earl smiled unpleasantly. 'I see. I knew it would come to this in the end. You're going to try to shake me down. Right? Well, you go ahead; you try selling it to someone else. You do that and you'll have the police around here knocking on your door and you'll be off to gaol before your feet touch the ground.'

'Oh really. And what do you think the police would do? What would they be able to prove? Absolutely nothing. The library couldn't prove that they'd been robbed because they've no idea the thing is there. What am I going to be charged with … stealing something that no one knew existed?'

Earl nodded. 'I see. So you think that no one would suspect you. Is that it? What about that woman who saw you trying to get away with stuff before; caught you putting things in your brief case. I reckon she's been put there to keep an eye on you. It seems to me that they're onto you already.'

'If that's the case then we'd better call it off right now, hadn't we?'

'You can call it off after you've done this one job for me.'

Harold shook his head. 'You know what, Earl. I think I might just leave that little book right where it is for a while. It's safe enough. Nobody but me knows where it is and nobody's going to stumble across it by accident, I made sure of that. So if you don't mind I might just have a think about this for a little longer before I make up my mind about the price or about who I'm going to sell it to or even if I'm going to sell it at all. You can keep that,' he said indicating the photocopies.

'Big of you,' Earl snapped. 'And if you think you can double-cross me now, you little worm, then I suggest you think again. I didn't go to the trouble of having you put into that job just for your benefit. I know you've already done very nicely out of the things you've taken out of there and flogged off to your mates in the trade. Now it's my turn for the pay off, so don't you try to pull the plug on our deal. You know what I do to people who try to do that.'

'Oh, yes I know,' said Harold. 'I've seen what you've done to your wife. You're a coward and a bully, Earl.' He paused. 'And you know what, I think I'm going to leave that little book right where it is … permanently. Or better still, hand it to the library as a gift … pretend I just found it. They'd be tickled pink and I'd be a celebrity overnight: the man who discovered Australia's first publication. I might even get a raise and a permanent job at the library.'

That's when Earl Wright stepped forward and hit Harold Coney hard on the side of the head.

*   *   *

It was more than half an hour before Pippa saw her husband's car emerge from the basement of the building opposite.

She rose, hurried over to the counter and paid for the two cups of coffee and the pastry she had consumed.

On the kerb she paused to make sure that Earl's car had disappeared then crossed the road quickly, head down, heading for the entry foyer to the flats.

When there was no answer to her knock Pippa reached into her purse and took out the duplicate key Harold had given her soon after their affair had started.

She pushed the door open and called: 'Harold. How did it go?'

She walked quickly through to the kitchen at the rear of the flat and was surprised to find that Harold was not there. She returned down the hall and entered the lounge, but it, too, was empty.

She was about to continue her search when she noticed that one of the wingback chairs had been moved off its usual spot. The TV set on the wall was also out of its usual alignment.

Then it was with a surge of panic that she noticed the blood on the carpet.

She turned and hurried over to the small table under the front window. She pulled open the drawer but the envelope containing the photocopy was not there.

Hurrying through to the bedroom she noticed that Harold's mobile phone was still by their bed. Harold would never have left the flat without his phone. She picked it up and put it in her handbag.

She hurried out into the hall and consulted the telephone directory, took out her own mobile and thumbed in numbers.

Pat Strong was sun baking on the deck off her second floor bedroom when the call came. She reached for her phone on a small table beside the low couch.

At first she did not recognise Pippa's panicky tones.

'I'm sorry for ringing you at the weekend, Pat, but something awful's happened. Do you mind if I come over? I know where you live.'

'Come as soon as you like, Pippa,' Pat said wriggling upright.

'Who was that?' demanded Hodgkiss who was standing at the bedroom door.

'That was Pippa Wright from the library. She's the assistant to the fellow in charge of the deaccessioning.'

'And why's she coming here?' Hodgkiss was peeved at the interruption.

'She didn't say … just that something awful had happened.'

'Is that what she said … something awful?'

'Yes, Hodgkiss, unless there's something the matter with my hearing … which there isn't.'

'Then it had better be really awful,' said Hodgkiss, 'because I was looking forward to you and I having a quiet afternoon together now that you're away at work all week.'

'Don't be selfish, Hodgkiss. I don't think Pippa's the sort of person to over-dramatize things.'

'What on earth makes you say that? You scarcely know the woman and what little you know of her isn't very encouraging.'

'Not very encouraging! What do you mean by that?'

'Well she's the assistant to someone who you believe you saw stealing books from the library … or trying to. Perhaps she's come to confess. Perhaps that's what's awful.'

'I doubt that very much. Now, Hodgkiss, I want you to go downstairs and put on the coffee. By the time that's done she should be here.'

And that's the way it turned out. The percolator was

bubbling happily just as Pat let Pippa into the building then met her at the door of the unit.

Pippa's tear stained face told Pat that something was very wrong.

'What on earth's the matter, Pippa? What's happened?'

'It's Harold. He's disappeared and I'm afraid something bad must have happened to him.'

'Why do you say that?' Pat asked.

Just then Hodgkiss came out of the kitchen carrying a tray with mugs of steaming coffee.

After introductions were made the three settled down in the lounge.

'I'm afraid something's happened to Harold because there were spots of blood on the floor in the loungeroom and the hall. My husband had been there to see Harold over … a particular matter and I was concerned that there was going to be a disagreement and I know that Earl can be very violent if he's crossed. I saw Earl leave and now there's no sign of Harold.'

'So you think that your husband might have attacked him?' Hodgkiss asked.

Pippa nodded. 'It certainly looks like it. I knew they were likely to have a disagreement. After I saw Earl leave the building I went straight across – I'd been waiting in a coffee shop over the road because I didn't want to run into him — and let myself in to find out what had happened, but Harold wasn't there and I know he didn't leave the building with Earl.'

'Have you searched the building?' Hodgkiss asked.

Pippa shook her head. 'There's not much to search. There's only the flat, and he wasn't there, then there's the fire stairs, the hallways and the car park downstairs, and I can't think why Harold should have gone down there because his car is always parked in the stree .'

'Do you mind telling us what was the subject of this meeting that your husband and your friend were likely to have a disagreement over? No doubt that is at the heart of the matter.'

'I don't think that's any of our business, Hodgkiss,' said Pat.

Hodgkiss was about to speak when Pippa cut him off. 'No, I don't mind telling you that at all. It was to do with an arrangement they'd made. You see Earl arranged for Harold to get the job of overseeing the library's deaccessioning programme because he wanted him to search the library to see if he could find a particular valuable book that Earl believed was there somewhere amongst the hundreds of thousands of books they have.'

'And does this particular book have a name?' Hodgkiss asked. '

'Yes. It's only a little book, no more than a pamphlet really. It's just called the Standing General Orders.'

'I think you mean the General Standing Orders,' said Hodgkiss. 'Published in 1802. The first book printed in Australia unless I'm mistaken.'

Pippa looked at him in surprise. 'Yes, that's right. It's a very valuable thing and Earl has been trying for years to get his hands on a copy.'

'And what made him think there was a copy in the parliamentary library? There are two known copies in the Mitchell Library.'

'He told me that someone he knew claimed to have seen a copy of it in the parliamentary library once, but then lost track of it when there was a flood in the basement and all of the books were moved about.'

Hodgkiss shook his head. 'That's not much to go on.'

'Perhaps not, but it seems he was right!'

'Really. How do you know that?'

'Because Harold found it.'

'Are you sure? If he did it would be the find of the century in the book world.'

'I know he found it because he made two photocopies of it; I've seen them.'

'And do you still have them?'

'Not both of them. Harold was going to take one of then to show it to Earl this morning just to prove that he had actually found it, then they were going to discuss the price.'

'So the book itself is still in the library?'

'Yes, but I've no idea where.'

'But your friend Harold knows where it is.'

'Yes, he does.'

'And the second photocopy; where is that?'

'I suppose it could still be lying around the flat somewhere.'

Hodgkiss turned to Pat. 'I don't like the sound of this, Pat. I think we had better take ourselves off to Mr Coney's flat without delay.'

'I'd be so relieved if you would,' said Pippa. 'Perhaps you could help find him.'

'Perhaps. But I don't like the sound of this, not one little bit,' said Hodgkiss.

His pessimism was soon to be vindicated.

*   *   *

Pippa led the way in her small sedan and Pat followed in her top-of-the- range silver Mercedes with Hodgkiss beside her, issuing unnecessary directions. When they reached the flats Pippa drove down into the basement car park and Pat stopped at the kerb where she and Hodgkiss climbed out and waited for Pippa to let them in at the street door.

'What time did your husband arrive?' Hodgkiss asked as they made a quick inspection of the flat.

'I suppose he arrived about ten. I was in the coffee shop over the road because I didn't want to be here when he arrived. He was here a little more than half an hour. I saw him drive away alone. He has an open sports car and he was the only person in it. Then I came over and when Harold didn't answer the door I let myself in.'

'And you haven't touched or moved anything?' Hodgkiss asked.

'No. What you see is exactly the way things were. You can see from the marks in the carpet that the chair is not quite in its usual place and the TV has been knocked skew-whiff. It usually faces straight into the room because we sit on the sofa over there to watch ... when we watch, which isn't often.'

'And you're quite sure that those stains in the carpet here and in the hall were made today. They couldn't have been there before, could they?'

'No, Mr Hodgkiss. I'm quite sure of that. Harold is a very particular housekeeper.'

'Then we'd better find the source of the bleeding, hadn't we,' Hodgkiss said. 'I assume there is some internal access to the car park.'

'Yes, there's a fire escape that goes down to the basement.'

Pat and Hodgkiss followed as Pippa led the way down a flight of dark cement steps which stopped at a fire door. Pippa pushed the door open and the others followed her into the basement.

Hodgkiss stood near the door, head down examining the concrete floor. Almost at once he set off towards a bay in one side of the parking area where a collection of recycling bins stood in neat ranks.

He stopped and turned. 'I want both of you to stay where you are, please.'

Pat was about to protest but Hodgkiss was already at the bins, raising the lids of the larger bins first and making a quick examination of the contents.

As he lowered the lid of the last bin he turned to Pat. 'Would you kindly ring home and ask Donald to get here as quickly as possible.'

'Hodgkiss, what is it?' Pat asked, alarmed as she thumbed her tiny phone.

'It's not good news,' he said hurrying back to where the two women stood. He took Pippa's hand. 'I'm afraid I have found your friend Harold.'

Quietly Pippa began to cry.

* * *

Detective Inspector Donald Burke was not amused.

He had been at home on a day off when the call came. Esme took the call in the kitchen and when she heard Pat's voice she had assumed that it would be news of her father who, these days, spent more time at Pat's unit than he did at home.

But as soon as she had heard Pat's urgent tones she knew that this was no social call and when she asked for Donald, Esme replied: 'Yes, of course, Pat. I'll get him for you right away.'

Esme hurried with the handset to Donald who was seated at the round redwood table on the back deck reading the local newspaper, *The Northern Star.*

'Yes, Pat, what can I do for you,' he asked cheerfully. 'I hope Dad hasn't been up to any mischief.'

'Well, I wouldn't call it mischief exactly,' Pat said cautiously. 'It's just that … well, there's no other way of putting it, but Edgar's found a dead body … again.'

There was silence as Donald processed the information. Then he erupted into rage.

'So what's he done now? Interfering again, I suppose. How often have I told him not to get mixed up in other people's problems?'

Pat began: 'Well, it wasn't his fault this time. It's a friend of mine, actually, and she …'

Donald steam-rolled over her. 'How often have I told him just to mind his own business. Again and again I've told him the same thing, but no, he just never learns. If someone tells him about something that sounds suspicious what does he do; does he tell it to the proper authorities? No, he has to start investigating it himself. He has to go poking his nose into situations that really have nothing to do with him.' He paused. His outrage exhausted.

'I'm sorry, Donald,' said Pat. 'I suppose it's really my fault in a way. You see I have a friend, Pippa Wright, and she …'

'Hold it 'til I get there. Pat. Where are you?'

When Donald arrived the three were waiting on the footpath. He made an effort at politeness while Hodgkiss introduced him to Pippa but his anger was barely diminished.

'You've done it again, haven't you, Dad?' he snapped. 'You just can't help interfering, can you?'

Hodgkiss did not attempt to offer a defence.

'So where's the body this time?' Donald demanded.

Without a word Hodgkiss, Pat and Pippa led the way down the vehicle access ramp to the car park.

Hodgkiss nodded towards the row of recycling bins. 'It's in the end one. The green one.'

'I suppose you took the trouble to make sure the fellow's really dead, did you?' Donald said over his shoulder as he strode towards the array of bins.

'I think you'll find he's well and truly dead,' Hodgkiss replied. 'I take it you've already called for the usual crime scene assistance.'

Donald did not bother to reply. After completing his examination he lowered the lid of the bin and turned.

'OK. Now who's going to tell me what happened? Pat, what do you know about this fellow?'

Pat replied. 'His name is Harold Coney, but I think Pippa's the right person to tell you about him.'

Donald turned to Pippa. 'Have you identified the ... um person in the bin?'

Hodgkiss interrupted. 'Really, Donald, that is the most insensitive thing I've ever heard; even from you. Don't you think your time would be better spent finding and arresting the person who did it rather than making callous demands upon innocent parties?'

'And I suppose you know who did it, do you? And where to find them?'

'As to your first question, the answer is yes; there is little doubt that the person who killed Mr Coney is Pippa's husband, Earl Wright.'

Hodgkiss looked to Pippa for confirmation. She lowered her head and nodded.

Hodgkiss continued. 'And as to where Wright is at the moment, that is of course a matter for speculation. I would think it doubtful that he has returned home although I suppose we should not rule it out.'

'And where's home?' Donald asked.

'Not far from here,' said Pippa. 'West Lillimoor, down near

the shopping centre.'

'And you think he might have gone there?'

Pippa shrugged. 'If he killed Harold I doubt if he would go home, not for long anyway. He'd know that the police would be looking for him as soon as the body was found.'

'Then have you any idea where he might go. Does he have any special friends who might try to hide him?'

Pippa shook her head. 'None that I know of. Earl was not the sort of man who made friends. He had no trouble making enemies.'

'Then you've no idea where he might be?'

'No, I don't, but one thing I can tell you, and that is he'll very soon be running short of money and he can't get his hands on any more without some help for me.'

'And why's that?' Donald asked.

'Because he's an undischarged bankrupt and his finances are extremely complicated. He can't do much in the money line without me being involved. He'd have a certain amount of cash with him and he kept a stash in the flat, but he can't put his hands on any real money except through me.'

'Then he doesn't even have a credit card?'

Pippa shook her head. 'No credit card.'

'That's a bit of a nuisance,' said Donald. 'We can often trace people when they use their cards.'

During this exchange Pat and Hodgkiss had been engaged in a whispered conversation.

Hodgkiss held up a hand. 'Donald. I think Pat and I might have hit on a way of flushing Wright out into the open.'

But Donald's anger had not yet fully abated. 'Oh, you might, might you? Then allow me to suggest that you leave police work to police officers. No offence, Pat, but I think you'd be the first to acknowledge that too often in the past

Dad has been too damned eager to demonstrate how smart he is; how much cleverer than the police, and it hasn't always gone quite according to plan. So on this occasion would you do me a favour and make sure that he doesn't get involved any further.'

But Hodgkiss was having none of this. 'And just who do you think you are, Donald, ordering Pat around. And as to my intervention in previous investigations of yours, I think it would be fair to say that my suggestions have often proven more productive than your bumbling efforts.'

'That's enough, Hodgkiss,' Pat warned. 'I think Donald's right. We should leave it to him from here on.'

'But I think our suggestion about involving Carol would definitely be the best course, so if ...'

'Hodgkiss. Enough!' Pat snapped. 'I think it's time we went home and left this to Donald. You come with us, Pippa, if you want.'

'Most sensible advice I've heard all day,' said Donald. He turned and retreated up the access ramp to join the crime scene officers and the police doctor who had just arrived amid a shriek of sirens.

'What was that you were saying about Carol Wales?' Pippa asked as they made their way back to the cars.

'Hodgkiss had an idea about how we might be able to flush your husband out of hiding. Do you still have that second photocopy of the General Standing Orders?'

Pippa nodded. 'I expect it'll be in Harold's flat somewhere.'

'Do you think you could lay your hands on it ... now?' Hodgkiss asked.

'I think so. There're only one or two places where he's likely to have put it. I'll see what I can do. Of course the police may not let me back in the flat. Meet you at your car.'

Ten minutes later Pippa emerged from the front entry of the flats with a large carry bag. She made straight for the Mercedes where Pat and Hodgkiss were waiting. She pulled open the door of the rear compartment and climbed in.

'No problem,' she said. She reached into the carry bag and came out with a brown envelope. 'Here it is. Same as the one Earl took when he left. What are you going to do with it? And how does Carol Wales come into it?'

'It's just an idea I had,' said Pat. 'I might be barking up the wrong tree altogether but Edgar and I think it's worth a try.'

Pippa sat listening for five minutes while Pat outlined their plan.

Pippa laughed. 'It's a long shot but I guess it's worth a try. We've got nothing to lose … except the second photocopy.'

*   *   *

On Monday morning the atmosphere in the parliamentary library was subdued.

The head librarian, Raymond Quilty, called an early staff meeting to draw attention to Harold Coney's absence.

'All I can tell you, and indeed all that I know, is that Harold Coney was the victim of a fatal criminal assault at his home some time on Saturday, probably in the morning, and that the police are investigating. I will keep you informed if I learn any more on the subject. I have no reason to believe that the assault was anything other than a random attack by some vicious criminal and that it was in no way connected with his work here. As you are all aware Harold was not a member of our regular staff but had been brought in from outside to assist with our deaccessioning programme which will now have to be suspended until a new person can be found for the task. I will be looking into that without delay. I have been contacted by the police officer in charge of the investigation, Inspector Donald Burke, and Inspector Burke has indicated that he may at some time during the course of his inquiries visit us here. What he hopes to learn from any of us I have no idea. I merely mention it to you in case he comes and asks questions. I need not tell you that you will be expected to co-operate fully with him.'

And that was that. The staff all returned to their stations and went on with their work.

Pat and Carol Wales entered the short corridor leading to their offices.

'Life goes on,' Carol commented.

Pat nodded. 'Did you know Harold very well?'

'Hardly at all. Of course he hadn't been here very long. But neither have I, come to that.'

Soon Pat was working on a fresh stack of old periodicals to be catalogued. About ten o'clock she rose and walked through the main office to the staff cafeteria next door. There, sitting alone at a small table near a picture window that looked over the Domain, she drank a mug of coffee and ate an iced fingerbun.

Ten minutes later she was back at her desk.

In another ten minutes she rose again, holding in her hand what appeared to be a flimsy document.

She took the five paces from her office to Carol's door, which stood open, and knocked.

When Carol looked up she stepped into the room and set the document down on the desk beside Carol's computer.

'What do you think I should catalogue that under?' she asked. 'Any ideas? I've never come across anything like it before.'

She noted the flicker of amazement on Carol's features.

Then Carol shrugged. 'I've no idea Pat.' Casually Carol reached out, picked up the document and transferred it to the other side of her desk. 'I'll look into it for you,' she promised and pointedly continued with her work.

Five minutes later Pat glanced across to the other office where Carol was on her mobile phone, hand raised confidentially to cover her mouth.

Pat smiled and went on with her work. Ten minutes later she took the mobile phone from her handbag and called up a number from the menu.

She said, *sotto voce*: 'She's taken the bait, hook, line and sinker. I gave her our little dummied-up copy of the General Standing Orders. When she saw it she damn near jumped out of her skin. As soon as I put it down on her desk she picked it up and moved it to the other side of her desk in case I decided I wanted it back to try to do the job myself. Then I'd no sooner come back to my office when she was on the phone almost straight away and had a very confidential conversation with someone or other. I suppose if Donald could do a check of her mobile phone records we'd soon know who it was, but I think we've a pretty good idea, haven't we?'

In his bedroom at the front of the Burke's bungalow Hodgkiss sat on the end of his bed, phone pressed to an ear.

'No doubt about that. But I wouldn't depend upon Donald for any help. Now that phase one of our little operation, the delivery, has been accomplished successfully we will now move on to phase two; surveillance. I take it you have Ms Wales' home address.'

'Yes. I took a sneaky look in Quilty's staff book while he and his secretary were at morning tea. She lives in a block of flats in East Rosbury not far from the station.'

'East Rosbury! How convenient. Now, you follow her between the library and the railway station, assuming she travels by train ...'

'She does. I saw her weekly ticket the other day when she opened her purse to pay for coffee.'

'Fine. And I'll be waiting for you near Rosbury Station and we can both take it from there.'

Pat had no difficulty following Carol from the parliament house building down to Wynyard railway station. Carol was so pre-occupied with calls on her mobile phone that she was almost knocked down by a cyclist as she crossed against the pedestrian lights at Pitt Street.

Pat passed through the ticket barrier immediately behind her and hastily turned her back when the machine refused Carol's ticket and she had to back out and try her ticket in another turnstile.

When the train came Carol found a seat inside on the lower deck and Pat stood on the upper deck for the short trip.

As the train approached Rosbury station Pat held back and allowed several other passengers to filter between Carol and herself as they alighted onto the platform.

At the station exit Hodgkiss, who had been waiting behind a public phone booth, stepped forward and took Pat's arm.

'Which is she?' he asked quietly.

Pat nodded in the direction of a young woman with long curly blonde hair who was waiting at the traffic lights on the Northern Highway.

'Let's hope she hasn't got a car parked somewhere,' said Hodgkiss.

'No need for a car I shouldn't think,' said Pat. 'She lives only three minutes' walk from here; the first side street on the left off the highway.'

But it soon became apparent that Carol Wales was not going straight home. When the lights changed she crossed quickly and entered a large coffee shop that fronted the highway directly at the traffic lights. Once inside she looked around then took her place in a booth opposite a dark-haired man who wore a thick drooping moustache of the kind favoured by certain cricketers in the seventies.

'That's our man,' said Pat. 'Tall, dark and a big moustache, according to Pippa's description.' She turned to Hodgkiss who was standing close beside her out of sight of the couple inside. 'What do we do now?'

'I think that's enough for today,' said Hodgkiss. 'I'd say that from now on it's going to be up to Donald. We've established a connection between your work colleague Ms Wales and the fugitive Wright. Donald would be justified in demanding that she tell him how she knew to contact Wright even if she doesn't know where he's hiding out at present.'

Pat nodded. 'Well, I suppose that's a start. So where do we go from here? My car's at the Grattan Station car park.'

But before they had decided on a plan of action Carol Wales and the dark, mustached man rose, he paid at the counter and the two left the coffee shop picking their way carefully over the uneven footpath, headed north.

'We might as well see where they go,' said Pat, setting off in distant pursuit. Hodgkiss fell into step beside her.

'Obviously they're going to Carol's flat,' said Pat, 'where she can show him the booklet ... our booklet. It's only a few minutes walk.'

Pat's speculation proved accurate. The other two continued along the footpath, turned left off the highway at the first side street then immediately around the corner they entered an old-fashioned two storey block of flats.

'I think we should contact Donald,' said Pat. 'If he hurried he could pick that fellow up now. Should I try?'

Hodgkiss shrugged. 'Better you than me. He'd take no notice if I suggested it.'

'That's because you'd be sure to say something to antagonize him,' said Pat thumbing numbers into the key pad of her phone.

'Nonsense. He's just too sensitive to criticism. Always has been. I remember when he asked if he could marry Esme I just happened to comment on the length of his hair and you should have heard the fuss. All hell broke loose. I was accused of being an old fuddy-duddy and of course Esme and her mother both took his part and it's been like that ever since.'

'And that's the way it should be.' Said Pat as she thumbed the keypad of her phone. 'No luck there. His phone's turned off.'

'Then I'll have to tell him about it in the morning,' said Hodgkiss, then added: 'You'll probably hear the shouting and screaming from your place.'

*   *   *

'Just what are you telling me, Dad? That you actually saw this Wright character in a coffee shop at Rosbury last night and you never let me know.'

Donald was livid.

He glared across the narrow table in the breakfast nook at Hodgkiss who was neatly decapitating a boiled egg.

'Pat tried to ring you,' Hodgkiss explained mildly, trying to lower the temperature. 'You had your phone turned off.'

Hodgkiss scooped out a section of white from the cap of the egg and nibbled at it.

Donald ignored this thrust. 'Can you just stop eating for a minute and tell me; where did he go when he left the coffee shop? Do you know that?'

'Of course we know.' Hodgkiss dabbed his chin with a paper napkin. 'We followed him to a block of flats in Ferry Road, just around the corner from the highway. He was with a young woman by the name of Carol Wales. I believe she lives there.'

'Really! So who's this Carol Wales and what's her connection with Wright?'

'Ms Wales works in a room adjacent to Pat at the parliamentary library and her connection with Wright ... well that's a little more difficult to explain.'

'Well perhaps you can tell me how she fits into this business.'

'I think you should speak to Pat about it, Donald. She tried to raise this particular matter with you when we were at Harold Coney's flat on Friday but you were not in a very receptive mood.'

'No. And for very good reason. I had a body in a wheelie bin to deal with.'

'Just the same, if you had paused long enough to listen to what Pat had to say you would very probably have Wright under lock and key by now.'

'Stop going on about it, Dad, and see if you can get Pat on the phone for me.'

'I think we should finish our breakfast then I'll see if Pat is prepared to lend assistance. After the way you treated her I shouldn't be in the least surprised if she told you to go to the devil.'

'That's enough of that, Dad,' said Esme who had been hovering uneasily at the stove, listening to the conversation with mounting concern. 'You know very well that Pat will do all she can to help Donald if she can.'

'I dare say,' said Hodgkiss stiffly. 'But that doesn't excuse ...'

'I said that's enough,' Esme snapped, and silence fell.

After he had hollowed out two boiled eggs and consumed two slices of toast Hodgkiss took the mobile phone from his pocket.

'Good morning, Pat. I must apologise for ringing you at this hour but Donald has decided, rather belatedly, that he would like to hear what you know about the relationship between Carol Wales and Earl Wright. If it is not convenient for you to speak to him now ...'

Pat was sitting at her breakfast bar, a mug of coffee in one hand. 'Of course it's convenient, Hodgkiss. Put him on.'

Hodgkiss passed his mobile across to Donald without comment.

'Sorry to bother you at this hour, Pat, but I can't get a sensible word out of Dad about this business.'

'Being his usual self, is he?'

'Worse than usual, actually. If that's possible. Now, I understand the two of you followed Earl Wright and this Carol Wales woman to a flat in Ferry Street near the Rosbury Station last night. Is that right?'

'Yes. I work with her and I followed her from work to Wynyard. Then I met Edgar at Rosbury station and we saw her go into a coffee shop opposite the station. Earl Wright was already there waiting for her. Then when they came out we followed them up the highway. They turned into Ferry Street and went into a block of flats. I'm pretty sure that's where Carol lives; bottom floor flat on the right. The light went on soon after they entered the building.'

'And what's the connection between this Carol woman and Earl Wright? Can you tell me that? Dad didn't seem to know ... or for some reason he wouldn't tell me.'

Hodgkiss, who had been following the conversation keenly, seemed about to interject but Donald raised a forbidding hand.

'Well, it's all rather difficult to explain,' said Pat. 'I happened to be standing near Harold Coney's desk one morning admiring the view from the big picture window in the main office. He was talking on his mobile to someone and I could hardly help overhearing what he was saying. The gist of it was that whoever he was talking to should keep an eye out for some particular item in the library. I suppose he must have thought that this item, whatever it was, might turn up among the things that Carol was cataloguing. He said something that made me think that he was looking for some document in particular but he wasn't at all sure that it was there anyway. He said: "Even so the bloody thing might not be here. No one's ever seen it that I know of. These are just stories." I'm sure he used those exact words. I made a point of remembering them because it sounded to me as if he had something definite in mind.'

'And you think now that Harold Coney actually found this particular thing.'

'Yes, he did. He photocopied it.'

'But when you overheard Coney on the phone how do you know that he was talking to this Carol Wales? Did you hear him say her name?'

Pat shook her head vigourously. 'No, nothing like that. I didn't think it was her at the time, but later I remembered that when I returned to my office Carol was on the phone too. It might have been coincidence I suppose. But she rang off shortly afterwards and I happened to notice that Coney, too, had ended his call at the same time.

'Anyway, because of what I had overheard I decided that Coney must have been telling Carol about the General Standing Orders and asking her to look out for it in the stacks of stuff she was being given to catalogue. I suppose that if it's anywhere it could possibly be among all the things they give us to catalogue given that it's all stuff that's been in storage undisturbed for ages.

'So Hodgkiss and I decided to test our theory. To do this we got Pippa Wright to give us the spare copy that Harold Coney had made of the standing orders and we made a little dummy booklet to look as much like the original as possible. Then on Friday afternoon I took it across to Carol's office, put it down casually on her desk and asked her advice about how I should catalogue it. She nearly fell off her chair. She grabbed it, put it down out of my reach on the other side of her desk and said not to worry, that she'd handle it. Shortly after that she made a very confidential phone call. Edgar and I figured that call was to Wright.'

But why Wright? What makes you think she even knew him?'

'It was pure guesswork mostly. I heard Coney mention his name in the conversation I overheard so I assumed that Coney told her about Earl Wright's interest in the thing when he was briefing her about the standing orders. If you want to be sure you'll have to ask her.'

'I'll certainly do that,' said Donald. 'Well, thanks, Pat. It's certainly much easier dealing with you than with certain other people I know.'

Hodgkiss grunted and wriggled awkwardly out of the narrow seat.

*   *   *

Pat was at her desk early the next morning. Carol Wales's office across the corridor was empty and the glass door was closed.

Ray Quilty put his head around Pat's door about 10 o'clock and asked if she had seen Carol, but Pat could only shake her head.

'It's not like Carol to be late,' Quilty muttered as he disappeared towards the main office.

About half an hour later Carol came in quietly, head lowered. She put her bag down in her office then crossed to Pat's room and pushed back the door.

Pat looked up. 'Ray Quilty was looking for you, Carol.' She noticed that Carol's make up had been applied heavily but even so it could not conceal a blackened eye.

Carol closed Pat's door and sat down in a visitor's chair.

'There's something I need to ask you, Pat; it's about that little pamphlet you gave me to catalogue.'

Pat sighed. 'I thought it might be.'

'You knew it was a fake then, did you?'

Pat nodded. 'Of course. A friend and I put it together.'

'Why? Why did you do that? It got me into the most awful trouble.'

'Yes. I can see that. I'm sorry, Carol, I really am. I had no idea it would lead to anything like that.'

'But why? I'm sure you didn't do it just for the hell of it.'

'No, we didn't. You knew what it was then, did you, that little booklet … you realised the significance of the General Standing Orders.'

Carol nodded. 'It was the first thing ever printed in Australia.'

'That's right. You knew that when I put it on your desk, didn't you?'

'Yes, I did. You probably noticed that I was surprised.'

'But you'd only just been told about it, hadn't you? Probably just a day or two before.'

Carol nodded.

'And it was Harold Coney who told you about it; how valuable it was and that you should keep an eye out for it in the things they bring us to catalogue.'

Carol nodded once more.

'And Harold also told you that Earl Wright, Pippa's husband, would pay a lot of money for it if it was offered to him.'

'That's right. Harold said if I found it we could sell it to Wright for a bucket of money.'

'Then after I dropped it on your desk you contacted Earl Wright and arranged to meet him. You met him at a coffee shop in Rosbury then the two of you went around the corner to your flat and ...'

'How do you know all this?' Carol demanded angrily.

'Because a friend and I followed the two of you to your flat.'

'But why? What did it have to do with you?'

'Did you know that the police are looking for Earl Wright? They want to question him about the murder of Harold Coney.'

Carol nodded slowly. 'Can't say I'm surprised. He's a nasty violent bastard. When I showed him the thing you'd given me he just laughed and said it was a crude fake and accused me of trying to cheat him ... and punched me in the face.'

'Do you know where he's living at present? The police would love to get their hands on him.'

Carol shook her head. 'I'm afraid not. When I rang him we arranged to meet at the coffee shop. When he left my place

I've no idea where he went and I was in no state to follow him. I'm sorry, but I've no idea where he's staying now.'

'That's a pity. He should be behind bars.'

Carol reached into her handbag. 'Do you want this back?' She held out the dummy of the General Standing Orders.

'Thanks. It'll be a souvenir of this business ... and a reminder to me not to make trouble for others.'

Carol stood up. She smiled. 'Don't worry about it too much, Pat. It's a good lesson to me too ... about being greedy.'

*   *   *

Donald was not optimistic. 'We'll have a helluva job to catch him now. He'll go to ground. He'll get one of his dodgy book-collecting mates to hide him until he can slip out of the country.'

Donald, Esme, Pat and Hodgkiss were having dinner at the round redwood setting on the back deck of the Burke's home.

Hodgkiss put down his spoon. 'Well, if you had bothered to come when Pat called instead of having your phone turned off ...'

'That's enough, Dad,' said Esme. 'You can't expect Donald to be on call twenty-four hours a day.'

Hodgkiss pronounced pompously: 'You don't have to make excuses for him, Esme. Any officer with real zeal and ambition would be only to glad to make sure that he was available whenever the occasion demands. I remember when I was teaching ...'

'Dad, I don't want an argument about it, thank you. Eat your dessert.'

'You know I don't like pineapple.'

'Really. That's the first time you've ever mentioned it. You've always eaten pineapple in the past and never complained.'

'That's only because I was always too polite.'

'You! Too polite!' Donald scoffed. 'That'll be the day when you're too polite about anything.'

The argument would have continued had it not been interrupted by the ringtone of Pat's phone.

'Yes, Pippa. What is it? What's the matter.'

Pippa Wright was whispering. 'I think Earl has come back … to the flat.'

'Are you sure? Where are you?'

'I'm outside. I've just arrived home from the shops. I can see someone inside moving around inside with a torch.'

'It's probably a burglar.'

'No. Whoever it is they've turned off the alarm so it has to be Earl.'

'Do you want to speak to Inspector Burke? He's right here with me now?'

Pat handed the phone to Donald. 'It's Pippa Wright. She thinks her husband has come back and is inside their flat.'

Donald took the phone. 'Hello, Pippa. Can you wait where you are and I'll be there very shortly. If he comes out don't try to stop him or follow him. I'm leaving now.'

Hodgkiss rose and followed Donald who was hurrying towards the short flight of steps leading down to the driveway.

At the bottom of the steps Donald stopped and turned. 'And where the hell do you think you're going, Dad?'

'I'm coming with you or course. And so is Pat.'

'You most certainly are not. If I need help I'll ring for proper back up … not you.'

'Donald, do not be obtuse. You are well aware by now,

surely, that both Pat and I are inextricably involved in every aspect of this case. Pippa is an associate of Pat's. Both of us have played vital roles in advancing the case to the point where you are now at last going to be in a position to make an arrest … assuming you don't bungle things at this late stage and it would not be the first time that you have managed to do that.'

'Don't you dare speak to Donald like that, Dad. Besides, Pat didn't say anything about going, did you Pat?'

'No, I didn't,' said Pat, 'but I must say that I'm very concerned for Pippa's safety. She said she's waiting just outside the flats. If Earl comes out and sees her there could be real trouble. He's a very violent man and he needs her if he's going to be able to get his hands on more funds. I'd say that could be why he's gone back there, to try to force her to do or sign something that will give him access to more money.'

'Then you'd better take Pat with you, Donald,' said Esme. 'And you'd better take Dad too, I suppose. For my sake, please Donald.'

Without a word Donald turned and stamped off angrily down the driveway towards the unmarked police car.

As they approached the flats Pat spotted Pippa Wright waiting in a side street around the corner from the flats. When she saw the car approaching she ran out to meet them at the kerb.

'I think he's still in there,' she said. 'I've been looking around the corner every few minutes and I haven't seen anyone leave and his car's not in the basement so he must be on foot which is hardly surprising because if he was still driving around in that sports car of his the police would've picked him up long ago.'

'Then let's go and have a look inside,' said Donald heading

along the footpath towards the flats. 'Do you have your key there?'

Pippa reached into her handbag and handed Donald a key. As they approached the flats they saw a light in Pippa's flat go on.

'Well there's someone in there all right,' said Donald. They followed him into the entry foyer and grouped around the front door to the flat.

Donald slid the key into the lock, turned it slowly and pushed the door open quietly. He raised a finger to his lips and began stepping silently down the hall, the other three close on his heels.

Then Earl Wright appeared in the kitchen at the end of the hall. They watched as he opened the refrigerator and took out a bottle of wine. With his teeth he twisted off the cap, raised it to his lips and took a mighty draught. It was apparent to the onlookers that this was not his first drink of the day.

Then he realised that he was not alone in the flat.

He turned and saw the four figures standing, crouched silently in the dim hall.

'What th' 'ell are you people doing here?' he demanded belligerently, swaying alarming. Then he recognised his wife among the group. 'And you, you bitch,' he said. 'And wovu done w' my cheque book?'

'It's not your cheque book, Earl, and I took it with me when I left,' Pippa called. 'Is that why you've come back, is it? You want me to sign some more cheques and papers for your shonky deals. Well, Earl, I've signed the last cheque for you. Besides, you won't need money where you're going.'

'And who are theesh people?' Earl demanded.

'The man in front is an inspector of police. He's come here to arrest you for murdering poor Harold Coney.'

'Poor Harold Coney,' Earl echoed derisively. 'He musta been pretty poor if he couldn't find himself a better root than you.'

Earl swayed so alarmingly that he had to grasp at the handle of the fridge to save himself from kissing the floor.

Donald stepped forward, issued the caution and applied handcuffs to Earl's compliant wrists.

With some difficulty Earl reached into an inside pocket of his jacket and took out a photocopy of the general standing orders.

'Here. You c'n have it back. 'S'no good to anyone,' he slurred. 'Bloody thing's a …' He pondered heavily: ' … a chimera.'

'A what?' Donald demanded.

Hodgkiss supplied: 'A chimera: ,, a fantasy or a daydream; a figment of imagination'

Earl pointed drunkenly at Hodgkiss. 'Give the ol' fellah a prize. A figment of 'magination. That's wha' they are … those standing orders. No such things.'

'I'm beginning to think he might be right,' said Pat. She turned to Pippa. 'I don't suppose Harold told you where he put the thing after he made those photocopies.'

'He said that he'd just put it back into the stack where he found it.'

'And that's all he told you?'

'I'm afraid so.'

Pat sighed. 'That's it then. It's gone … and this time it's probably gone forever.'

*   *   *

'Hodgkiss I'd prefer it if you didn't keep ringing me at work. I think I've told you that before.' Pat was sitting in her tiny office, mobile phone pressed to an ear.

'You've mentioned it several times in fact, but this time it's important … or fairly important.'

Hodgkiss was sitting in the captain's chair in front of the computer in his bedroom.

'All right. Tell me whatever it is, but please, make it snappy.'

'It's about the unlovely Earl Wright. Donald just rang to tell me that Wright's confessed to killing Harold Coney.'

'Well that's hardly a great surprise, is it? I expect they found plenty of scientific evidence. It was hardly a carefully planned murder, was it?'

'No. That's what Wright said. Donald said that he's agreed to plead guilty to manslaughter. Reckons it was an accident. And you'll be fascinated to learn that the General Standing Orders actually helped contribute to his downfall.'

'Oh. In what way?'

'The scientific boys found Wright's fingerprints superimposed on top of Coney's at several point on that photocopy.'

'Hardly conclusive,' said Pat.

'Well, according to Donald it was one of the factors that helped convince Wright to confess.'

'Very interesting, I'm sure. Now, Hodgkiss, if that's all, I've got a mountain of work here to get through.'

'I see,' Hodgkiss said stuffily. 'All I can say is that you have very strange priorities. Apparently communicating with me now rates lower than the discharge of a totally unnecessary task which you perform at considerable inconvenience to yourself in order to earn money that you don't need. Do you realise that you are working mostly for the benefit of a government that shows its appreciation by refusing to extend to you even the meanest benefits which it insists upon showering on many far less deserving citizens.'

'What a rant!' Pat exclaimed and cut the connection angrily.

Hodgkiss scowled, rose and set off for the back deck where he settled in one of the uncomfortable director's chairs and took from his shirt pocket the chess puzzle which he had clipped neatly from the weekend papers.

Ten minutes later he had just found the solution, a waiting move with the white king, when his mobile, which he had set down nearby on the redwood table, buzzed.

He reached over and snatched it up. 'Yes. What is it?' he snarled without looking at the caller's number.

So he was amazed to hear Pat's voice again.

'I really don't know why I have anything to do with you, Hodgkiss,' she snapped. 'I've always detested rude people.'

'Well you can hardly blame me for being a trifle testy. Last time we were speaking only a few minutes ago you hung up in my ear.'

'I did nothing of the sort. We had finished our conversation.'

'You may have finished. I most certainly had not. As I recall I was reminding you of the way in which you treat, or should I say mis-treat ...'

'Save it for later, Hodgkiss. I've got some news for you.'

'Indeed. Then I hope it's more interesting than ...'

'Hodgkiss! Be quiet! It's about the General Standing Orders.'

'Is it? What about it?'

'I've found it. I'm holding it in my hand right now.'

'Nonsense. You can't be.'

'I might have known you'd say something like that.'

'Where did you find it?'

'I didn't find it. The young fellow who brings me in bundles of things for cataloguing just put a new stack down on my table and it was the third from the top.'

'But how do you know it's not a fake. There're fakes and copies floating around as you well know, having created one yourself.'

'And I was not unaided in that unfortunate little exercise, was I? But I promise you there's no chance this is a fake. It's old, it's dirty, it's scribbled on … it's the genuine article, Hodgkiss, I'm sure of it.'

'I dare say you are, but don't you think I'd be the best judge of that. You have no expertise whatever in such matters. Why don't you just pop it into your bag and bring it home and we'll have a proper look at it tonight. Come over for dinner.'

'But I've had dinner at your place three nights in a row.'

'That's all right. Esme doesn't mind.'

'Whether or not Esme minds is hardly the point. Besides, how do you know she doesn't mind? Have you asked her? Of course you haven't, you never do, you just take it for granted that that poor woman will fit in with your every whim, the same as you do with me.'

'Don't you think we're rather getting off the subject? If you don't want to come here for dinner I'll see you at your place or I'll meet you at a restaurant somewhere. It makes no difference to me.'

'But I can't simply put this thing in my bag and walk out with it. If anyone caught me I'd go to gaol. This is a very valuable document, Hodgkiss, or have you forgotten that.'

'It's only valuable if it's the genuine article … which it almost certainly isn't.'

'But it is. I'm sure of it.

'Pat, as I have already pointed out you are no expert in old documents. It needs to be verified by someone who knows something about the subject.'

'In other words, someone like you.'

'Yes. Now, will you do it … please?'

'And if you decide it's real … what then?'

'Ah. Then we'll have to give it some serious thought.'

Pat frowned and looked down at the small, shabby document. She shook her head. What on earth should she do?